HIDING FROM CHRISTMAS

Off-the-Grid Christmas Book 1

MARYANN CLARKE

About Hiding From Christmas

Hiding from Christmas
(Off-the-Grid Christmas: Book 1)

He's been hiding from the world since he lost his family in a brutal attack.
She's just hiding from her family for the holidays.

What happens when they find each other?

Elle

I couldn't face the piteous glances of my family over the holidays after my fiancé Austin unceremoniously dumped me. I was too tame, too awkward, too vanilla, too risk averse. Glad he took five years to figure that out.

I'm devastated. Humiliated. And angry. I told Mom I couldn't bear the thought of coming home for the holidays. I'd rather be alone. Anything was better than their sympathy, but my own company didn't promise to be any better. That's why I jumped at the chance to visit my eccentric aunt Muriel in a remote village on the West coast of Mexico.

Joe

No one would call my solitary life here uncomplicated, but on the surface it's simple enough. After seven years in exile, I'm used to my routine and my solitude, though my grief walks beside me like a silent companion. As much as I might like to go back to my old life, I could never put the people I trust, love and depend upon at risk.

Never again.

I'm regularly reminded that the cost would be too high. Especially this time of year when a cruel gift arrives from my nemesis. My sixth Christmas alone in Mexico. The anniversary of the date I lost everything.

I'm expecting the package, right on schedule. But I'm not expecting the clumsy, beautiful, bewildering blonde that crashes into my world and turns it inside out.

Praise for Hiding From Christmas

Unexpected romance
Hiding from Christmas: Off The Grid was an unexpected story. This story was interesting, drama filled, and a bit steamy…This story has drama, romance, a bit of violence, and keeps you on your toes.

Unique Romance
Hiding From Christmas is a fantastic and unique romance filled with fun, emotion, suspense, danger, and steamy chemistry…I highly recommend this superb romantic suspense.

Fun and unexpected!
I really enjoyed this book… I loved Elle's character because I could relate to her! Joe was an interesting character. He made me laugh. The romance, steaminess, and adventure made for a really fun book! It's not your typical Christmas story and I appreciated it being different!

Perfect holiday read
This is just what I needed. I absolutely loved every second of this

amazing book. If you're looking for a fun, sexy, feel good romance that will grab onto all your emotions then this is the perfect book . I read so many dark romances that it was a welcome change to have a smile on my face throughout the entire book.

Hiding From Christmas: Off-the-Grid Christmas
This is the story of two people who find love while batting anxiety, heartbreak, and deep emotional pain. One is in seclusion due to a broken relationship and the other one from tragedy and self imprisonment. It's a well written book with tons of emotions, suspense and danger. The author had me glued to the pages right to the end as she delivers an entertaining story.

Rom-com
Funny heart warming rom-com. Enjoyable characters, entertaining plot and interesting side characters make for an afternoon of fun reading!

Multi-layered
This story has numerous storylines that are seamlessly connected. Elle starts off with such poor self confidence while being self deprecating. I hurt for her. Joe is in hiding for an extended period of time with excellent reasons. This fractured couple help heal each other. The way this story flows and the pacing are smooth and engaging.

Chapter 1

ELLE

IT'S ALWAYS BEEN my misfortune to be a misfit. Awkward, bookish and shy, I set my sights early on modest life goals. Perpetually being knocked back on your keister will do that to a person.

The toe of my sandal caught on a rough edge of paving stone and I tripped, stumbling and dropping my cloth beach bag, the contents spilling among the agave and poinsettias in Aunt Muriel's wild terrace garden. How strange to find the iconic Christmas flower growing in her yard rather than in foil wrapped pots at the supermarket this time of year. For sure, this would be a strange holiday, the first I'd ever spent away from my claustrophobic family.

Gathering up my sunblock, novel, notebook and water bottle, I pondered how my clumsiness and awkwardness were both literal and metaphorical. It seemed I was forever tripping, dropping, bumping, falling and making messes, physically and socially. And being laughed at. Left behind. Not chosen. Not…special.

A long, defeated sigh whooshed out of me.

At thirty-four, I was used to that. I was self-sufficient and realistic. Still, my dream of being special to someone, at least one person, was slipping away like beach sand through my fingers. And with it, my hopes and dreams of love, family, and my own modest kind of happy ending.

Everyone in my life was a successful over-achiever. I may not be super successful like my sister the dentist, or wildly popular like my brother with his music history podcast. Or just plain good at everything like my younger cousin Tannis, who was super smart, athletic, musical, beautiful and popular. Thoughts of Tannis, though we were close and I loved her intensely (being left out of so many games and outings as a tween left me her *de facto* babysitter growing up) made my stomach clench and turn over. She set such a high bar I would always look like the poor, hopeless, hapless cousin Elle, next to Tannis.

Or even just sweetly perfect like my dear friend Laura, whom everyone loved. She was good at everything too, in a gentler sort of way. A talented designer running her own interiors firm, engaged to the perfect man—handsome, successful, charming–— she was the star of her family and circle of friends.

And then there was me.

Part of me was fully aware that I was knee deep in a wallow of self pity, I just happened to think it was well earned, in this case. I knew I wasn't a bad person, or a completely useless one. I had strengths and applied them well. Like at work, for example. I'd found what I loved and was great it. My job as an elementary school teaching librarian gave me purpose. Finding the perfect book to awaken literacy and a love of reading in every child, no matter how unique brought me joy every day. My students loved me. And I loved them. All children, really, were my delight. Sadly getting to know all the terrific kids at school was a painful, daily reminder of my own fruitless dream of a family. One that, at my ripening age, and in my freshly single status, I might never have.

My co-workers loved me too, even though they never let me use the paper cutter, or climb the step ladder to hang decorations because, well everyone knew how that would turn out. Still, my job was the one bright spot in my life.

My personal life, not so much.

I'd always tried so hard to pull myself together into a package that people would like. Respect. Admire. I made careful decisions and choices, moved with precision, tried to be kind to everyone, took care with my appearance, trying to be neat and stylish without offending anyone. Yet I was always found lacking.

For Austin, my boyfriend of four years and fiancé the last two until two weeks ago, it had been my lack of adventurous spirit. I admired that about him, with his passion for glacier snowboarding, mountain biking, hang-gliding, mountain climbing and any other dangerous, high-intensity sport ——he was a risk junkie really—— and the gorgeous athletic body that made all of that possible, of course, along with his fun-loving personality.

I'd never asked him to give up the lifestyle he loved, only to reduce the risk he put himself into, for the sake of my poor heart. Yet he expected me to run and jump and fly alongside him, though it just wasn't part of my make up, and I couldn't fake that kind of courage and recklessness. Not even for Austin, who I loved, and who I'd thought loved me.

But he hadn't loved me, not the real me, as it turned out. Like everyone else in my life, except maybe my students, he wanted me to be something other than what I was.

I couldn't face the piteous glances of my family after Austin unceremoniously dumped me. By email! From his extreme frisbee tournament in Munich, abruptly announcing that he wouldn't be home for Christmas (he'd be skiing with friends in Switzerland instead) Nor did he want to marry me after all. Irreconcilable differences, he'd cited, made a life together unthinkable. Adventures awaited him and his joie-de-vivre. I was too tame, too awkward, too vanilla, too risk averse. Glad he took four years to figure that out. Not!

I'm devastated. Humiliated. And simmering with well-behaved anger. I told Mom I couldn't bear the thought of coming home for the holidays. Both Laura and Tannis were busy this year. I'd rather be alone, but my own company didn't promise to be any better.

So here I was in a remote village on the West coast of Mexico. The not-quite-unwanted house guest of my eccentric Aunt Muriel, whose invitation came at just the (suspiciously) right moment to save me from the ribbing or worse, the blatant pity of my parents, siblings, and cousins, all through the holidays. I suspect Mom might have twisted Muriel's arm.

Pausing on a large flat stone patio halfway down the hill, in the midst of Aunt Muriel's lush tropical garden, I spun slowly, taking in the vista of beautiful turquoise bay, and marveling at the glorious trees that grew right outside her door. Avocados, mangos, papaya, lemon and lime, date and coconut palms, over a lush flowering undergrowth of bright red shrimp plants, orange zinnias, and other spiky exotic looking things.

My gaze tipped up to peek at Muriel, her bony shoulders hunched over her old fashioned *manual* typewriter on the open breezy deck under the shady fringe of palm palapa fronds that roofed her little house. Her face was hidden in shadows under the wide brim of her straw hat, but in my mind's eye, I could still see her frown of concentration as she tap-tap-tapped away at her current manuscript. A warm, gregarious hostess she was not. We weren't close, but though most of my family considered her stranger and more wretched than me, I'd always admired her for her sharp intellect, her independent spirit and her strength of character.

Even my eccentric aunt whose hospitality I was currently testing had achieved a certain measure of success as a mystery novelist.

I thought, perhaps, staying with her would give us a chance to bond. We had books in common, at least. But Muriel made it quite clear upon my arrival that I would be neither pitied, coddled, nor waited upon. She said there'd be some kind of informal potluck gathering of ex-pats and friends on Christmas Day, but she expected me to entertain myself the rest of the time so she could work on her book.

Being an unwanted house guest at my reclusive spinster lesbian author aunt's tropical estate wasn't exactly what I needed. On the other hand, I had successfully escaped from the miserable ruins of my life and didn't have to slouch around at my parents' house feeling like a flat fifth wheel now that my supposed husband-to-be had cut and run.

I envied Muriel. She didn't need anyone to be content, and I wished to be more like that. Stronger. Self-contained. More resilient. Giving Muriel the space and privacy she was accustomed to, and expected, wasn't a problem for me. I needed plenty of time alone to think.

Or wallow in self pity, as the case may be.

When I got to the bottom of her rocky steps where they met the main walking path, I paused again. The village, and the beach, with its few shops and cafés, were a rather long trek to the right past dozens of ex-pats' alternately humble and sometimes quite elaborate homes tucked between the palms and pines and higher, on the bare pale rocky hillside flanking the two riverbeds, like a settlement out of Swiss Family Robinson on the Mosquito Coast.

At the north end were the public beach, busy boat launch and obnoxious crowds of tourists. There was no better place to feel utterly alone than in a throng of happy holiday revelers. Especially at a beach filled with vacationing couples and noisy families, everyone festive for the holidays, including the locals in the tiny village itself where tinsel streamers and star shaped paper piñata were being hung from the simple cinderblock and Palapa building frames, and Feliz Navidad scratched out of some old record player on an infinite loop while skinny dogs snuffled around in the dirt.

Muriel had warned me off of going in the other direction. "There's nothing out that way, and if you fall down or drown there'll be no one to save you," she'd grumbled, clearly wanting me to, at the very least, stay out of trouble.

Yet I eyed the narrow, ill-used path, a strip of dusty fine beige sand along a rocky ledge gently lapped by the turquoise sea. It was not an inviting path, possibly quite treacherous beyond the bend, and yet it held far more appeal than the prospect of being alone among strangers.

I began to pick my way to the left, the vague notion that, despite the rocky terrain and steep hillside rising beside it, I might come upon a narrow sliver of sand. All the beach I really needed to spend my solitary day. I did want to swim and soak up the lovely tropical sun, after all, and I had to occupy my days somehow while staying out of Muriel's way.

JOE

A STEADY BEEP from my computer woke me from a damned good afternoon nap, warning me that something had breached my perimeter security fence again.

Flipping through the security camera views, scanning the boundary of my remote acreage, I finally discovered a fallen tree branch on the property had broken through my electric fence down near the beach trail. Damn it! Probably that storm last night. I was in a bad enough mood this week already. At least it wasn't intruders this time. I'd had to deal with enough foolish teenagers and stupid tourists in the past. I flipped off power to the system, preparing to head down to make repairs. That was the downside of living alone. When a job needed doing, you had to do it yourself.

The upside? Nobody bothered you.

Sometimes, after weeks and months of solitary same-same, I began to wonder if the electric fence was designed to keep everyone else out, or me in. Trapped in a prison of my own making.

Reluctantly lashing sandals onto my usually bare feet, I gathered my canvas bag of tools, grabbed my shotgun from its locked case and stomped out of my sprawling open air house, across the terraces and gardens, and down into the bush to fix the broken fence. People didn't tend to come poking around much nowadays. I'd scared them off years ago. But it paid to keep everything up to scratch. The tropical jungle had a way of getting ahead of you. It was not fond of man's attempts at civilization.

As I made my way lower into the thicker jungle at the bottom end of my property, I stopped in my tracks to listen, crouching low. Something, or someone crashed through the bush just out of sight, and my pulse kicked up with a jolt of adrenaline at the thought of an actual intruder.

ELLE

I JOLTED awake as cool waves sloshed over my ankles and up my shins. Squawking, I bolted up off my beach towel, scrambled to gather my belongings and jogged a short way up the sand, out of reach of the rising tide, laughing.

How long had I snoozed in the hot sun? I touched my arms and shoulders, feeling the heat radiate off of tender overdone skin.

Having ventured along the narrow, forbidden path for fifteen minutes, I'd come upon a tiny bit of sand nestled in a dip in the shoreline, a few feet wide. Convinced I could do better, I continued along the ever-narrowing path a further ten minutes or so, eventually clambering carefully around the rocks until I came to another indentation at the base of a small valley where two ridges came together.

A beautiful, secluded white crescent of sand between two large rocky outcroppings stretching into the sea like dragons' tails, providing me with such a perfect, private place to spend my days I felt like I'd found a pirate's treasure. I'd found what I'd been looking for.

It was so exquisite I wondered why Aunt Muriel hadn't told me about it, in fact had expressly told me not to venture this way. Perhaps in her mind I needed the noise and festivities of the crowded beach and town.

But this… this is what I'd come to Mexico in hopes of finding. Exactly the balm my wounded soul needed. I was happy to have found this secluded spot not so very far beyond my aunt's house. I would come here every day and spend my time alone and soon my heart would heal and I could go home and start my life again.

Snow white sand shone through the translucent turquoise water and I'd been suddenly desperate to swim. I dropped my cover up and towel and slathered on more sunblock before swimming in the crystal clear aquamarine water, as warm as a bath, for a long luxurious time.

Relaxed and satisfied, I'd lain on my towel and read my novel until drowsiness overtook me. Then, I suppose I'd gone out like a squelched candle flame. Probably, I'd have a nice sunburn to show for it.

I sighed and turned my gaze out over the sliver of beach and let my eyes rest on the gorgeous pale turquoise water stretching out to the edge of the bay with the hazy purple coast spanning from one side to the other as though they were two lovers who could not quite join their hands together across the divide. But in the arc of their reaching arms the bay undulated gently with the rising tide.

Then I suddenly realized that the path I'd used to get here was gone. Covered by several feet of sea that crashed against the steep rock outcrop with a white violence that concerned me. Looking up, I saw that those lazy dragon tails rose to a sharp-spiked dorsal spine. Climbing and crossing it in my flimsy sandals would be treacherous, if even possible. The tide continued its relentless climb closer to the shore, which, after a rough stone bench, rose steeply into thick jungle.

In the moments I'd stood hesitating, the tide had reached my feet again and I stepped back further, the available surface narrowing rapidly.

I'd have to give the rocks a go. But after only a moment of scrambling and slipping, my hands and shins were scraped and bleeding.

Sighing, I reassessed the jungle. Along my walk, I'd passed a few discrete pathways leading up the hill to houses where no one was welcome. Or if those people had friends I don't know who they were. Surely there'd be a way up this hill, too, despite the dense jungle that crowded the edge of the beach. Edging along the embankment, I peered into the shadowed, tangled greenery of mangroves and date palms searching for a way through.

And there it was. Barely discernible, a little used path, just over the low swing of a sideways growing trunk.

Trapped, literally, between a wall of sharp rocks and a very hard place, I chose the hard place. Sweeping aside the wide, flat fronds of date palm, I stepped over the tree trunk, hoping I didn't encounter any scorpions. At the thought, a shiver ran up my spine. My aunt had said that during the heat of the day they tended to hide in cool moist crevices, just like this place, so I watched carefully where I put my feet to make sure that I didn't accidentally step on one.

This was just like me. I'd managed to get myself into a scrape yet again.

The brush was overgrown and I had to push aside palm leaves and prickly shrubbery to continue along the path. Clearly it was never used.

Suddenly I had to pee rather urgently, probably because of the shift from hot sun to cold water to hot sun to cool shade. That, and nerves, were making havoc of my insides. Still, I could see a little bit of blue green sea behind me, so I ventured further. I looked around and decided this was as private a place as any to take care of my business before curiosity carried me further on.

Not much farther into the jungle, the path changed. It widened, and I could see that the foliage had been trimmed back to ease the way. So someone used it after all. Perhaps I'd even find a house at the top.

Of course the very next thing I noticed was a crude sign nailed to a tree.

PROPIEDAD PRIVADA
   SIN TRASPASO

MY SPANISH WASN'T great but I understood that. No trespassing.

· · ·

IN SMALLER PRINT underneath were the additional words: *Los intrusos serán fusilados*. I was less sure what that meant, but '*fusilados*' did not sound good. Chuckling nervously, because surely they didn't mean it literally, I carried on. I had no choice.

Beyond the sign, the path became more groomed, with steps cut into the steeper parts of the bank.

I came to a wire mesh fence strung between round poles with no evidence of a gate. Strange. It was neatly and well made, but a few yards over, it was broken. Two poles leaned, and the wires had been pulled down by a large fallen branch creating a breach. I flicked my bag at the wires to make sure they were not electrified. Just my luck to be jolted with electricity all alone in the middle of the Mexican jungle. It seemed to be fine so I carefully stepped across the fallen wires into the brush beyond, working my way back toward the path.

I'm not sure why I kept going, except this mysterious path was too intriguing to ignore, like the children's adventure books I read to my students. The Chronicles of Narnia or Bridge to Terabithia. What might I find? I could simply wait out the tide closer to the shore, though it would be a long wait before I'd find my way back. Maybe I'd discover an old abandoned house. It could be my private retreat, a place I could come during the day to read and sun and stay out of my aunt's hair when I wasn't actually swimming.

The scrubby wilderness thinned slightly, spreading out between taller trees, allowing red flowering bushes to thrive in between. Glad to be out of the tangled damp jungle, I came to a stretch of rocky terrain where big boulders had formed a kind of shelf around three feet in height, with a pleasant looking plateau above. I scrambled up onto the ledge, was just righting myself when the sound of a rifle cocking next to my ear froze me to the spot.

A gruff voice barked, "Stop right there." In English.

Heart racing, I scrambled to apologize. "I'm sor–"

"What the hell do you think you're doing on my property!"

My words of apology stuck in my throat. I stood, slowly, turning toward the rifle barrel six inches from my neck.

A startled scream left my throat before I even saw him, my hands flying to cover my face.

"Can't you read?"

I raised my wide eyes to the terrifying beast of a man behind the gun, swallowing. Wild looking, with long, untidy brown hair, a thick ragged beard, he glared at me with startling blue eyes like sharp crystals. My gaze scanned his baggy, ratty cargo shorts and worn leather sandals. His wide shoulders and shirtless chest were broad, sculpted and tanned. Even more buff than Austin, and a thousand times more dangerous.

The instinct to escape was so primal I lurched backwards with a cry of alarm, too late realizing there was no ground behind me, flailing my arms as I lost my balance and tumbled backwards off the stone ledge.

"It's a damned good thing I was doing maintenance on the security system today or that fence woulda zapped–aw, fuck!"

Crashing into the underbrush, my head hit a hard surface with a sharp, painful *crack* and everything went dark.

Chapter 2

JOE

FUCK ME.

MY RAGE at the intrusion drained away rapidly as I took in my intruder. I glared down at her nearly naked form waiting for her to get up and run away. But she didn't move. She just lay there limp, her limbs twisted this way and that her mouth slack.

"Get up," I barked. "Get off my land." But she didn't move. Shit shit. She was unconscious. She must've hit her head falling backwards. I scrambled down over the stone ledge and bent over her. I checked over her arms and legs, felt her neck, looking for broken bones. When I slid my hand beneath her head to lift it, I felt the sticky heat of blood. Damn it! Pulling my hand away I saw that she had indeed knocked her head against a rock beneath it. All I needed. A corpse on my property. I checked her neck for a pulse, relieved to find it.

Fuck. How did this happen? She must've crossed the fence just when I turned the electricity off. It had only been ten minutes for God's sake. Now what was I going to do with her? I couldn't leave her lying here in the jungle. The insects would get her if nothing else. And that was assuming her injury was minor and she didn't need medical attention. Fuck!

I set down my rifle and scooped her limp form into my arms, then bent to pick up the gun and tramped up the path towards my house. The last place I wanted or should be bringing a stranger.

Up the steps through the open living area to my sleeping area behind the floating wall. I grabbed a towel on the way and tucked it beneath her bleeding head before moving to set her on my bed. The bed, hanging from ropes to keep the scorpions out, swayed back and forth as I leaned against it.

Before I could set her down, she lifted a limp hand to her head. "Oohh. My head." Then it flopped back down, landing on my bare chest.

I jerked back at her murmured words. She was conscious! Thank God.

"You're so strong, Austin," she mumbled, bringing a frown to my face. She was delirious, thinking I was someone else. Her hand stroked my chest, curling over one shoulder, sending devastating sensations careening through my body.

"Uh. Hey," I tried.

Instead of opening her eyes and seeing me, she nestled her face into the crook of my shoulder, sweeping her hand around my neck and over the skin of my back. I rolled my eyes to the palm thatched roof overhead, grunting. This couldn't be happening.

"Thank you for rescuing me, Austin. I love how athletic and manly you are." She continued mumbling, her lips pressed softly against my neck, her voice as light as a breeze. "I'm so glad you understand I can't do the reckless things you want me to. I'm not built that way. I need you to be the strong one." She let out a long breathy sigh, humming softly, tickling my skin and sending lustful signals south. "I can't help being afraid, baby. I'm afraid for you, too. I love you and couldn't bear it if you got hurt." Then her hand dropped and she went limp again.

I cleared my throat. "Hey, miss. Hey!" But that was it. She was a rag doll again as I set her on the mattress and stepped back. I took a moment just to look at her, taking in her long slender limbs, her sun-kissed pale curves, her mess of golden curls, coiled into dark ropes from being wet. The strap of her prim navy swimsuit top had slipped over her shoulder, and the triangle of fabric covering her right breast hung loose, giving me an almost unobstructed view of her beautiful curving chest. My own flesh sprung instantly to life, standing proud and excited in my shorts. I hadn't seen a woman, let alone a nearly naked perfect one up close for years. Never mind touched a woman's soft skin or held her in my arms. So many years I could hardly blame my cock for jumping to attention at the novelty. She was as different from my wife had been as could be, and yet I felt certain, even in normal circumstances, I'd find this one desirable.

Lord, help me. I had to do something about her bleeding head. I fished through my storage cupboards and pulled out bandages and cloths and disinfectant. I wetted a cloth and returned to her. Still completely out cold.

I had to get her up and get rid of her as quickly as I could. It was bad enough that she had seen me at all, but I could only hope that with the shock and trauma of it all she wouldn't even remember me. I sat beside her on the bed setting it swinging again, a deprived part of my brain traipsing down a fantasy lane, imagining crawling onto the mattress to tangle my limbs with hers, setting my mouth on her silky skin. Being this guy Austin that she admired. I shook the image from my head. *Put that ridicu-*

lous thought out of your head, Joe. There's no place in your life for that nonsense.

I pushed her by her shoulder onto her side so I could see her wound. Blood was already congealing and drying on her light hair. I tried to wash it away as much as I could so I could see the gash. It was deep enough to bleed profusely, but looked like a surface laceration. Certainly her skull was not cracked open. Thank God. That's all I needed was to have to call the chopper for something like this. I did not need that kind of attention. As a foreigner, her injury like this on my property would draw the attention of the authorities.

I rinsed the cloth and cleaned her up a bit more. Smearing on some antibiotic ointment and covering her wound with soft gauze, I wrapped her head in a strip of folded cotton tying it off neatly at one temple.

I stood up sighing heavily, scratching and scraping one hand over my tired face. Quite the day. I'd have to leave her here and continue with my fence mending. I couldn't leave the gap untended, nor the power off or I'd have all manner of intruders wandering on my property.

As I strode back down the hill I thought about the half-dozen invaders I'd had to deal with in the past seven years. At first it was locals, curious kids or workmen looking for new contracts. But they soon learned that they were not welcome, and even so my defences grew stronger with each invasion. At the beginning one or two of the ex-pats had made overtures of neighbourliness, but I had soon dissuaded them as well. Now everyone knew better, if they thought of me at all. Just the way I wanted it.

I thought about the beautiful woman lying unconscious on my bed and wondered where the hell she'd come from. This far from the village and the boat launch, I virtually never saw anyone I didn't already know, at least by sight, since in fact no one knew me, and I knew nothing about them except what I could infer by spying through my binoculars. This woman must be someone's guest, or else a very intrepid explorer looking for adventure. Certainly from her reaction to me, and from her delirious words, she did not seem to be the latter.

Whoever she was, I had to get rid of her before she ruined everything.

Chapter 3

JOE

AFTER MAKING the necessary repairs to my fence, and turning the charge back on to keep anyone else from ruining my day, I returned to my unwelcome guest. This breach of security was unprecedented in all the years I'd been living here. Somehow, I had to get rid of her before she figured out who I was.

She remained insensate, no more murmured talk of her hero Austin. I wasn't sure if I was grateful that she hadn't woken up again and started snooping around my house in my absence, or more worried that she was still out cold.

She was a very attractive woman, perhaps a few years younger than me. My chest squeezed with a deep, crippling sense of loss. Loss of my wife, my family, loss of the life that I knew, though those feelings were old and dulled like rocks beaten by the constant crashing of the sea. Simply the loss of human contact. Still, I felt it like a cavern in my chest. My solitude. My loneliness. The appearance of this woman in my space after all this time shone a bright light on my miserable existence.

Standing over her, lying there on my bed, I could not stop my imagination from running amok with what my eyes beheld. I couldn't get over the fact that the mere presence of a woman in my space was so disorienting. I had truly become a miserable old hermit. And again my cock stood at attention, expecting me to do something with the beautiful stimulus before me, despite my rational mind insisting that it stand down.

With a grunt I exited the main building and stripped off my shorts at the threshold of my outdoor shower. I was accustomed to taking care of my basic needs, on a nearly daily basis. What else was a hermit to do? It's the life that I had resigned myself to. But standing naked with tepid water sluicing through my long hair, streaming over my hot dusty sweaty skin, my gaze cast out over the turquoise sea beyond the treetops losing focus, the very image of that woman's form in my mind's eye drove my need to new heights. Almost against my will, I turned and squinted through the woven slats in the screen separating the bathing area from the bedroom, catching just the shadowed outline of her curving feminine form prone on my bed, like the pervert that I apparently was. With just two or three strong strokes of my fist, I reached my release with such force that I had to lean against the stone enclosure wall to hold myself upright. I disgusted myself and pitied myself. I had to get rid of her and fast before I did something foolish.

Chapter 4

ELLE

EVEN BEFORE I opened my eyes, every cell of my body registered that I was in a place I'd never been before. That strange sensation sent adrenaline shooting through my chest, setting my pulse thrumming with anxiety. How could that be? The last thing I remembered was—

Oh.

A fragmentary image of the scowling wild man, furious blue eyes flashing like lightning bolts with the wrath of a Norse god, blinked in my mind.

I shot up with a gasp, my eyes wide, primed to flee, but before I could take in the foreign surroundings, or a path of escape, shooting stars exploded behind my eyes, and a tropical thunderstorm crashed into my head. The resultant pummeling pain, like a million children's feet stomping on my brain, dropped me prone to the pillow again, moaning, eyes clenched tight against the onslaught, hands clutching my head.

Oh, dear.

I encountered a bandage wrapped around it and froze. Where the heck was I and where did the wild man go? Obviously I'd hit my head. Had he brought me here? Tended my injury? My mind wouldn't fit the pieces of this disorienting puzzle together into a picture that made sense.

I squinted one eye open to see what I could see. I was on a big bed, somehow suspended from the beamed ceiling by thick ropes. The air on my skin still carried the heat of the day. Above me, the typical thatched palm frond roof, just like my aunt's palapa house. Without moving my head, I swivelled my eyes back and forth and caught glimpses of heavy dark wood furniture, a dresser or wardrobe of some kind, and an open doorway in a half-height white plastered wall. Not much to go on.

A grunt, like an animal barking, interrupted my reconnaissance.

I stilled, listening. Was that a dog? A ... a ... I drew a blank, my mind scrolled, trying to recall what sort of wildlife lived in this part of Mexico, mostly from children's books I'd read. Basically I came up with skinny dogs. A monkey? An opossum?

The sound of water trickling, which I had not previously noted, stopped abruptly, replaced by some quiet shuffling sounds, and the twittering of birds in the trees outside. I felt him. He was right there. The man.

I kept my eyes shut tight. Maybe if he thought I was sleeping, I could wait for him to leave and sneak away. Assuming I could lift my head and get up. That remained to be seen.

One way or another, I had to get out of here. Whoever he was, he didn't want me here anyway. But now that I was here, would he help me get home? Or... why did he bring me here anyway?

My pulse thrummed as I pushed aside myriad terrible thoughts.

Suddenly I felt him come closer. He stood right there, a few feet away from the bed. Breathing.

What was he doing? What should I do?

Again, without moving a muscle, I cracked open one eye, attempting to see him.

There he stood, in the middle of the room. Stark naked! His long brown hair and tangled beard hung in wet tendrils, dripping water on his broad tanned shoulders and sculpted chest and stomach. He held a towel and absently ran it over himself, catching the water droplets. My view slowly traced the dark trail of hair and water that marked the centre line, incapable of stopping myself from seeing … everything.

Including the admirably sized cock he ran his large hand over, then stroked with the towel in his other hand, lifting it higher for my perusal as he dried himself. My lady parts clenched with involuntary need and want at the sight of his impressive appendage, and I closed my eye, feeling bad for spying on him. I'd missed Austin's attentions this last few weeks, and this guy had what I had a hankering for.

In another situation, I might have swooned at his astonishing physique. He was tall, well-proportioned and built like a carved statue of a Roman god, all his muscles articulated and bulging with power. His wide chest tapered to narrow hips over thick thighs like tree trunks. Ordinarily, he was exactly that kind of spectacular athletic male that got me tingling with want and faint with desire.

But not right now. Not him.

I peeked again. Those muscles demanded attention, insisting that I run my hands over their tempting hills and valleys, turning me into a wanton, hormone-crazed teenager. Wasn't that true for every woman? I didn't know, but it was true for me, and my besties Laura and Tannis agreed. We were all huge fans of Channing Tatum, Hugh Jackman, Henry Cavill and the Rock. It was my great misfortune to be helplessly attracted to big, strong alpha men. Like Austin. Like … this guy, despite his terrifying wild appearance. Although he did bear a striking resemblance to Jason Momoa, now that I thought about it.

Did that make me superficial? Was I a bad person? I couldn't help being attracted to a certain type of man. People had types, right? I sighed and squirmed, perhaps with a bit of misplaced longing.

In this context? What was I thinking? I pushed aside lustful thoughts just as he took himself in hand, giving himself a squeeze and two or three long slow strokes with his fist, taking his half chub erection to full majestic mast. With a grunt, he stepped closer to me and tossed the towel onto a chest at the foot of the bed.

Oh, my God! I flinched. He froze and turned towards me, bending over.

What was he doing? Was he going to attack me? Was fate playing a joke on me? Was I to become the captive sex slave to a gorgeous deranged hermit? I couldn't be in a more vulnerable situation.

The mix of emotions swirled in my brain, sent confusing, conflicting feelings coursing through me. Overwhelming lust, quickly subsiding, mingled with uncertainty and fear, overlain with sadness at the loss of my own personal Adonis. Austin and I had a good thing. That's why we planned to get married after four great years together. We got along well, made each other laugh, took care of each other. We certainly had a satisfactory sex life. We made each other happy. I'd thought.

Why did he have to end it? Stupid selfish Austin! I hated him with every fibre of my being. Why did I have such terrible luck with men? The men I found attractive either didn't notice bland vanilla me, laughed at my nerdy awkwardness, dumped me, or were angry brutes who would take any female and—

Would what?

I had to get out of here. I had to get away from him.

I jerked upright, immediately clutching my head at the burst of smashing pain like grade school band cymbals. With a cry I fought it, scrambling back on the mattress to get further away.

"Please don't hurt me. Let me goooo!" My voice came out shrill and mewling through my tight throat. My heart lodged there, clamouring like a marching band. Tears welled in my eyes, clouding my vision.

"What? What the fuck?" He growled, the perfect deep gravelly sound to accompany his enormous, scary, distractingly beautiful body. He lurched toward the bed, and I screamed, covering my eyes and scurrying across to the far end of the bed, clumsily sliding onto the cool concrete floor. *Oh my God. Oh my God.* He's coming for me. My heart raced and my head pounded unrelentingly, drowning my vision in flashes of red and black fireworks, knives slashing at my eye sockets. It was unbearable.

"For fuck's sake, woman. I'm not goddam attacking you," he barked.

But it was too late for me to register his words or calm my racing panic. I curled on the floor behind the bed, trembling, covering my splitting head with both arms, squeezing my eyes tight against the barrage of pain and fear and hysteria.

"Get away! Get away!"

"Hey. Hey, get up from there." He stepped around the foot of the bed and bent over me, his barking voice softening. *"Pincho estúpido.* What do you take me for?"

He reached down and gripped my arms, pulling me up from the gap behind the bed. I was rigid with fear, stiff as a corpse, but he lifted me as if I weighed nothing, and set me gently on the bed, crawling over me to get to the other side without letting go of me, as if he thought I had the power to run away.

Instead, I stayed curled up in a ball, whimpering, weeping, certain I was about to be harmed in some unspeakable way, paralyzed by fear and the pain in my skull.

He sat next to me on the bed, running his big warm hand over my legs, hip, shoulder.

"Shhh. Settle down, kitten," he purred, stroking, and I began to calm down. "I won't hurt you, you ridiculous woman."

Able to breath again, I opened my eyes and lifted my head to look at him. Still wild and scary, damp, and nearly naked, because he'd wrapped his towel around his hips, huge and muscled, yet the expression in his brilliant blue eyes was soft, kind, gentle.

I stayed closed up tight and rigid while his giant hand stroked my forehead, adjusted my bandage, tucked my hair back, brushing it gently over my shoulder. He began to hum a tune that seemed familiar. I was trying to place it when he added soft, murmured lyrics to the song.

"Lavender blue, dilly, dilly. Lavender green…"

I stared, mutely up at his kind face, his sad eyes looking back at me, his brow folded in concern. He was a gentle giant. An extremely sexy gentle giant. I was in so much trouble.

"You—" I croaked, but before I could say more, the floor tilted and the bed spun, my vision fading to black as I went limp in his hands.

JOE

SHE BLACKED OUT, the tension draining out of her. My God she was hysterical. I didn't realize she'd awoken or I'd never have been walking around nude, never mind ogling her like a pervert. I was about to get some clothes on when she went ballistic, clearly assuming I had ill intentions.

My gut clenched at the thought.

I might deliberately chase everyone away, but I was no brute. The truth was I was a sad, desperately lonely loser with a hopelessly broken life. The degree to which I was quickly becoming obsessed by this delicate, beautiful woman frightened me a little. It made me realize how far I'd fallen, beyond grief and fear and caution, into a numb sort of semi-existence.

Suddenly having her here in my space, my alternate worry about her lying there vulnerable and weak, possibly with a serious head injury I was doing nothing about, and her waking up to delirium, tears, fear and panic, had my emotions in an unfamiliar twist, a roller coaster, jerking between one feeling and another that I had pushed away for so long they were strangers to me. I felt my hard defensive shell crumbling and my nerves shattering.

It was overwhelming to have another human being near me. One that I could see and smell and touch. Not only that but she needed me, needed my care and protection in a way no one had for a very long time. I felt compelled to touch her, care for her, soothe and heal her. I'd have done anything to calm and reassure her that she needn't fear me, scrambling for anything I could do to convince her. Some buried instinct led me to pet her, stroke her, even sing lullabies to her. It was either soothe her like I'd soothe a child, had soothed my own children, or else pull her into my arms and hold her, kiss her like I had my wife. Somehow I didn't think she'd appreciate the latter even though that's the kind of soothing I needed.

As she slept, I caught myself staring at her for long moments, just drinking in her vulnerable beauty. Her femininity. Her humanity.

I'd missed so much.

Part of me knew I had to get rid of her, quickly and efficiently, which as I had the thought sounded nefarious. I meant her no harm, in fact despite my defiant body's shocking response to hers, she was vulnerable and frightened, and I would try to help her. I couldn't not.

And anyway, she was not yet well enough to make her way home alone.

Furthermore, she'd seen me. Seen enough of my home to compromise my security. Somehow I had to talk to her. I had to calm her down, heal her, befriend her and explain to her how critical it was that she never speak a word about me or this place to anyone. And in order to do that, she had to trust me.

She posed no threat to me, at least intentionally. But unwittingly, she could be a threat by sharing information. I'd be certain not to reveal personal details, meanwhile, or actually ravage her, which is what my sex-starved body demanded I do like the wild man she seemed to think I was.

And when it was safe to do so, I'd send her away, even though the thought of being alone again broke my heart.

Chapter 5

JOE

THIS TIME, she slept for hours. Which was good. She was healing and would be able to leave soon. But I began to worry that she would become dehydrated, or perhaps had had a concussion or a brain bleed and wouldn't wake up at all. My mind spun with the repercussions of such an event. Having to bring in the authorities to remove a body seemed exponentially worse than calling in a doctor.

My bad day was quickly becoming a nightmare. What was I going to do with this woman, and how long would it be before I could get rid of her? I thought about calling Luis and just getting him to take her away, but I knew that the arrival of the helicopter off schedule would only draw attention that I didn't want or need. Still, we touched base almost every day, by text if not by video chat, and I'd have to tell him eventually.

With a vague notion troubling the back of my mind, I sat down at my laptop and logged on, realizing I had to let my right-hand-man know about the security breach, since he'd see something on the footage and call me anyway. I could only imagine what he would have to say if I told him about bringing the woman home after keeping my domain impenetrable for seven years.

"Hey, Boss," Luis answered.

I gave him the basic facts about the storm and fallen branch, about making the repair on the fence. At the last minute, I decided not to say anything about the woman. Something in me wanted to hold that a secret for a while longer. In case Luis offered to swoop in and take her away. Something in my gut held me back.

He grunted in acknowledgement. "Any other news?"

I narrowed my gaze at his face on the screen, skeptical. "Nope. This is enough of an upheaval for one day." I paused, pondering my options. It occurred to me that part of her hysteria might in fact be my appearance. Aside from the fact that I'd inadvertently walked in on her stark naked sporting a stiff shaft while assuming she was still asleep, which could not have helped matters much. My hair and beard had gotten very long, as I hadn't had to deal with anyone for very long time. I wondered if this was part of the problem.

"Hey, Luis."

"Hmm?"

"Tell me the truth. Do I look… bad? Scary?"

I wasn't expecting his guffaw of laughter in response. "I thought that was the point of all that hair. To keep people away."

"Hmph. Well, maybe I've let it go too far?" I drew a circle in the air around my face. "Is this horrible?"

"Well, I…uh."

"Why didn't you tell me, you fucker?"

He laughed again. "Doesn't matter to me, Boss."

I grunted.

"So otherwise you okay? Need any special supplies? A new razor? New suit?"

"Fuck off." I signed off and sat a moment, thinking, then returned to my bathroom. Certainly the tangles were a nuisance and I wouldn't miss them if I cut a bit off. If I cleaned up a little I might not be so scary when she woke up. Then maybe she'd listen to me instead of screaming her head off.

Normally I kept no mirror and I had no occasion to look at myself, nor care one whit what I looked like. What I saw in the mirror, that I could recall, were the eyes of a man broken by grief and guilt and that was a sight I didn't need to see every day. I was alone, I was always alone, and I had no intention of ever being anything but alone.

But I knew I had one somewhere. Rummaging in my cupboard I came across a small mirror, wiped its dusty surface clear, and set it against my toiletries shelf squinting to see what she saw.

It was a shock to be sure. Knowing your hair is long and your face is bearded is one thing but seeing the picture was something else. I looked like a wild mountain man from some mythic tale, and combined with my nudity, and before that, my rifle aimed at her, I felt a twinge of sympathy toward my unwanted guest. I think even I would've been frightened by the sight.

Well, I could do something about this. So while she slept I clipped and shore until I found my face again underneath all of the hair. I left enough beard to preclude actually having to shave. There's only so far I was willing to inconvenience myself for a stranger who'd be gone in a few hours, a day at most. When I saw my beard in the wastebasket the site was jarring. Like Rip Van Winkle, I had been here a long time. Rather than attempt a real haircut I simply chopped off my long tangled locks just above my shoulders, as straight as I could manage. Then I combed it neatly back and tied it with a band. That should be better.

Then I went to the kitchen to rustle up something to eat.

Chapter 6

ELLE

THE SECOND TIME I awoke it was to the delicious scent of cooking food wafting through the space. I was warm, relaxed and comfortable. My stomach grumbled in response and I realized I was parched with thirst, and starving. How long had I been here?

The light was blue and dim. Carefully lifting my head, testing its limits, I stretched to peer out at the sea over the wall, beyond the trees, trying to discern the time. The sun had set. From sounds and smells, I'd figured out I was in a bedroom loft of sorts, and the rest of his house lay below the half plaster wall that shielded it from view, yet allowed me to glimpse the trees and ocean beyond. I wondered if aunt Muriel worried where I was, or was so lost in her writing that she hadn't stopped to think about it. As this was not uncommon I decided not to fret too much. I was a grown woman and I'm sure she trusted me to make my way back.

Still, if I were to return home along the narrow rocky

seashore, assuming the tide was sufficiently low, it was far too dangerous in the dark. Despite my wishes, my second attempt to sit up was worse than the first and I ended up flat on my back again, hoping the room would stop spinning, and the black and red flashes in my field of vision abated before my empty stomach tried to heave.

Then he appeared in the open doorway at the top of the stairs. Without speaking he stared at me, and I stared back. At some point he'd covered my nearly naked body with a light woven Mexican blanket, and for that I was grateful. I clutched the soft striped cotton, pulling it to my chest, and looked him up and down.

He was dressed again though that seemed to entail a pair of shorts and no more. My gaze slid over his broad, tanned, contoured chest, his wide shoulders and bulging arms. The raw desire coursing through my veins was an embarrassment. Had I no pride? Somehow since I'd last woken up he'd lost his beard and half of his hair, and I stared at his unfamiliar face, puzzled at my wanton attraction to this stranger.

"You cut your beard," I croaked, my voice hoarse from disuse, or perhaps my marathon screaming bout.

His hand came up to feel his face, rubbing it as though he'd forgotten, and his dark brows came down in a scowl. "I did. I thought perhaps the way I looked had frightened you."

In a little kitten-like voice I confessed, "It did rather."

"Sorry about that." He looked around, gnawing his cheek, seemingly at a loss. "Made something to eat. Imagine you're hungry."

My stomach grumbled loudly at his words.

"I am, actually, very."

He nodded, one cheek twitching minutely in what I thought might be a flash of amusement. He stood solid as a mountain, considering me for a long moment before he spoke again. "How's the head?"

I reached to touch the bandage again. "Sore. It hurts when I try to get up, and I'm very dizzy and weak."

He scowled. "I'll bring you plate so you don't have to move too much." And he disappeared down the stairs. Five minutes later he returned with a tray, the image incongruous. He stepped forward and set it on the edge of the bed beside me. I looked down to see a bowl of steaming chunky broth topped with thin shavings of corn tortilla, and diced avocado.

"Tortilla soup?" Had he made this himself? "It's my favourite. Thank you."

"Taste it first before you thank me. I'm used to my own cooking, but you might not like it."

"Can you prop me up a little?"

Grunting, he approached the bed, taking a second pillow and gently tucking it beneath mine to raise me up a few inches. "Thank you.

I lifted the spoon and scooped a taste of broth, with a little chicken, tortilla and avocado together, bringing it to my mouth. I tested the temperature and slurped it up greedily.

"It's delicious, one of the best I've ever had." The idea that this mountain man was a good cook danced in my head, looking for somewhere to settle.

He grunted in acknowledgement, and then just stood there watching me, unmoving. Self-conscious about eating in front of him, a stranger, upon whose hospitality I had imposed after invading his obviously treasured privacy, I waited. Studying me a moment longer, he nodded abruptly and left me alone to eat.

"I'll check your head after," he mumbled on his way out.

Chapter 7

JOE

LEAVING her with the soup to eat, I opened my computer to check for messages from members of my staff. A shipment of supplies wasn't due for another few days, but I was running low on a few things.

I wondered whether to ask Luis to take her away, rather than expect her to walk out of here in her condition. It would be kinder in some ways, but then where would he take her? If she went to a doctor in PV, she'd have to make her way back to wherever she was staying, and clearly she didn't have money or identification with her as she'd just gone off for a walk and wandered off the path. I had to watch her for awhile, get to know her a bit, before I could decide what to do with her.

I checked my email inbox for updates. Primarily these were of a business and financial nature, simple reports on suppliers, shipping schedules, orders, profits and losses. And my investments. I also checked in with my security team just to make sure that nothing new had happened, and no one had been making inquiries about me personally. These days that was rare. The press had long ago lost interest in me, along with the reading public. It was enough that I was known as the reclusive CEO of my company, and that no one ever saw me personally, as long as my people continued to conduct business as normal.

But there had been occasional instances of foul play over the years. It had never been clear whether these had been isolated occurrences of corporate mischief, simpler crimes of a random nature, or investigative forays by my enemies. In any case no one had ever found me, and I intended to keep it that way.

I thought again about the woman. There was, I suppose, a slim chance that she was a spy, a well disguised one. But I felt that I was a good enough judge of character to see through such a sophisticated ruse. She'd have to be damn good that's for sure. Besides, there was the head wound, which was real enough. So even though I didn't think that was likely, still I had to be cautious and keep an eye on her while she was here.

Clearly someone was at their desk, because not five minutes after I sent out a couple of emails, my phone dinged with an incoming message.

Luis: Hey, Boss.

Me: Anything to report?

Luis: Busy time of year.

He meant more than an increase of orders for the holidays. I waited, and sure enough.

Luis: Some Christmas mail arrived at the warehouse.

I sighed. Of course it had. It was that time of year. I dreaded the end of December. Just when everyone else fell into a frenzy of decorating, baking and shopping, or escaping for winter holidays in the tropics, I'd receive a solitary package.

Every year for the past six Christmases the bastard who killed my family, and tried to kill me, sent a prettily wrapped Christmas present. What would it be this year?

Me: Send it with the next drop.

Luis: I don't have to. Maybe I could take care of it for you.

Me: Send it.

Luis: Putting together your supply order. Any special requests?

Me: Not really. Why?

Luis: Wondered if you'd heard about the missing tourist?

Oh fuck. Already? I had hoped she was someone no one was paying attention to. No such luck.

Me: Oh? Where? Here?

I hoped that playing dumb would give me time to talk to the woman, win her confidence, and send her away quietly.

Luis: Yes, there. A woman is asking around the village. So I hear.

Me: Unlikely I'd see her, way out here.

Luis: I don't think I mentioned it was a woman.

Fuck me.

Me: I assumed. Bring extra tortillas and chicken. And maybe some...clothes?

I never could keep a secret from Luis. And technically it was unwise to do so since he was my head of security and everything else. But maybe I could keep this intrusion to a minimum without involving him. I had to try anyway. On the other hand, I should have asked for condoms. How did I get to a place in my life where I didn't have condoms.

Luis: Be careful. Let me know if there's anything I can do to help.

ELLE

WHILE I ATE, relishing every bite, I thought about my enigmatic host. Somehow, despite my earlier terror, he felt less like a captor, less of a threat. He was oddly gentle, shy even, cautious and nurturing, in direct contrast to his imposing form. The soup was so delicious, the chicken fresh and tender, the tortillas authentic and handmade, I wondered how such a man had learned to make such good soup. I wondered whether he kept his own chickens as many of the other locals did, both the Mexicans and the ex-pats who lived in this remote village on the side of the mountain by the sea. I could more easily imagine him killing chickens than tending them and gathering eggs. I wondered if he bought his tortillas from a local woman as my aunt did or even pressed them himself from the masa flour.

I also wondered that he'd chosen to remove his facial hair, ostensibly for me and my comfort, after but one encounter, when he had clearly not been motivated to do so for a very long time. Was that creepy? Was his attention to my injury, and my bodily needs weird or was it sweet? Until I knew something about the man I couldn't answer that. Maybe I could ask a few discrete questions.

He came to take away the tray and dirty dishes. After eating the soup, I was flat on my back again, my head throbbing. Perhaps I should have been worrying about the wound on the back of my head. I had tentatively felt around and discovered dried blood and considerable tenderness and swelling, but could learn no more.

He returned a few minutes later with a bowl and a cloth. He wet the cloth and wrung it out, washing my face and hands while I watched his face, curious and stimulated. Rather than the menace I'd imagined in my hysteria, he was in fact my rescuer. He didn't ask for me to barge onto his land and make a nuisance of myself, depending on his kindness for my survival. Yet he'd accommodated me. I was warming towards him in more way than one, his gentle touch rousing tingling sensations both over the surface of my tender skin, and throbbing deep in my core. I imagined his hands gliding over more of me, my breasts and thighs, and felt my nipples contract and my centre clench with need. I let out a shuddering breath. *Get a grip, Elle.*

"Are you cold?" he murmured softly.

"Huh? Oh, uh, no. I'm fine," I said, my voice deceptively breathy with my dirty thoughts. I rubbed away the gooseflesh on my arms.

Tamping down concerns for my safety freed me to openly admire his rugged handsomeness, though he was considerably more refined now that he'd removed some of his wild hair. His striking blue eyes still directed a piercing gaze my way, but now they felt wary and full of interest rather than blazing with anger. It made me wonder if his first reaction to me hadn't been motivated more by fear than rage at my invasion.

Who was he really?

"Just relax and I'll hold you up," he said in his soft, gravelly voice as he tucked his hair behind his ear and slid his big arm beneath my shoulders, gently lifting me, his other hand cupping my head so I needn't hold it up. I knew he was only nursing me, but the contact of his warm skin on mine, the solid feel of his muscled arm against my soft back, the clean masculine scent of his freshly washed body and the feel of his hot breath against my hair, turned me to quivering mush. Tilting me forward a little, he gently removed the wrapping bandage and lifted what I assumed was gauze.

Gasping, I flinched at the sudden sharp pain.

"Sorry. Sorry," he whispered, sucking air through his teeth. "It's stuck to your hair with dried blood. Hold on."

He wrung out the cloth and pressed it, warm and wet, against the back of my head, then leaned back and dropped his chin, peering into my face, assessing. "There's a gash back there, where you landed on a rock. I didn't think you needed stitches, but we'll see if it's still bleeding once I clean it up, okay?" His voice was gentle and calmed me as the pain subsided and the warmth of the cloth soothed me, water trickling down my neck and back.

"How do you know I don't have a concussion? Or a brain bleed?"

"I think we'd have a clue by now. You won't be here long. You can go to the clinic in PV."

I nodded my head slightly, meeting his crystal blue gaze. "If I'm still conscious." We were so close, a breath apart, and hot dangerous awareness flashed in his eyes, sending an echoing thrill through my body. My nipples tightened, and my inner muscles clenched in response, and I think he somehow felt it. He cleared his throat, swallowed loudly and dropped his gaze, rinsing and wringing out the cloth. I watched as blood swirled into the bowl, mixing with the water in eddies and clouds.

To deflect from the heated moment, I asked, "Did you happen to see my beach bag? Down by your fence?"

He grunted affirmative, pointing with his chin to the floor beside the bed. "It's here." I heard him drag it closer with his foot.

"Thank you."

We fell into a companionable silence as he continued cleaning my wound and my hair, gently dabbing and rinsing.

"How's your head feel?"

"It hurts like heck. Are you sure I don't need stitches?"

"I've cleaned the wound and had a look. It's a doozy of a laceration but narrow. I think it'll heal up okay. You're damn lucky your head didn't crack open like a melon."

"Oh yes. Lucky indeed."

He chuckled, a low warm rumble in his wide chest. "You're the one who was trespassing."

"Hah! How was I supposed to know that?"

"Oh I don't know. Electrified fence. No trespassing signs. Enter at your own risk. That sort of thing."

"For your information, Señor Important, I saw no signs," I

lied. "And the fence was not electrified. It was laying flat on the ground wide open on a path that looked like nobody had walked on it for the last hundred years."

He chuckled, the corner of his wide mouth quirking up in amusement. "Settle down, before you blow a gasket and start bleeding again."

I scowled at him, jutting my chin and pouting at the injustice. "I would not have dared to trespass if there had been any other way for me to go, but I was trapped by the rising tide. Furthermore, for your information I was only going to relieve myself and leave again when you scared me half to death."

"Yeah, sorry about that. Everyone knows better than to come here."

"Except tourists," I stressed, "of which this village gets its fair share, judging by the number of people disembarking at the boat launch."

"Those people stick to their day at the beach, and a very few venture to the village. No one but locals come this far down the path."

"Till now."

"Till now," he agreed, amusement in his voice, as he continued to dress my wound, wrapping a new bandage around my head to hold it in place. He tied off the bandage and lay me back on the pillows. A moment passed during which we both eyed each other, taking a breath and letting out some of the stress and resentment of our forced proximity.

"Where do you get the electricity for your fence anyway? And these lights." I gestured around the room. "Muriel has only a couple of solar panels and batteries for emergencies. It's all kerosene lamps and candles over there. She even uses an old manual typewriter."

His face twitched. "I have a lot of land." As if that answered my question. He stood and picked up the bowl of bloody water and old bandages. "It's late now." He lifted his gaze and scanned the horizon beyond the boundaries of his house. "Sundown. You'll have to sleep here tonight."

As if I had the strength or wherewithal to get up and walk the rocky shore back to Aunt Muriel's house.

"Maybe we can wash your hair tomorrow."

Wash my hair! That sounded so intimate, my gaze flew again to his, and I swallowed. I'd be spending the night here. In his house. In his bed.

"I…um. I don't want to impose on you any longer."

His massive shoulders shrugged. "No way for you to leave yet. It's not safe. And you need to rest."

I had many questions for him, but I had the feeling he would be reticent with the answers. Something about him, something about the way he lived, made it clear he was a man with many secrets, and possibly enemies. Either that or he was a madman and I was in trouble.

Chapter 8

ELLE

LYING STILL, listening to him move around, washing dishes and cleaning up, I tried to stay calm and think rationally. There was no reason to assume that his kind attentions were motivated by some creepy stalker-ish intentions. I'd watched too many suspense movies about serial killers.

As if laughing at my absurd, paranoid thoughts, he began to hum a tune. The same tune, I realized, he'd hummed and then sung to me earlier, to calm me down. Not a song, but a lullaby. One I'd learned at school from recordings of traditional children's songs.

"Lavender's blue, dilly, dilly, Lavender's green." He hummed the rest, while I tried to recall the lyrics, the dishes clinking as he stacked them. The metal bowl clanged. Water ran from a tap. He continued humming as my mind filled in the words.

When I am king, dilly, dilly
You shall be queen

Who told you so, dilly, dilly
Who told you so?

My heart pinched, my eyes filling, thinking what a lovely partner and father he would make. I didn't know why I thought so, but I knew it. Or at least I would love a partner who was strong and protective, yet gentle and sweet. Maybe it wasn't too late for me to find love after Austin. Maybe there was still someone out there for me. A divorcé, maybe. Someone like him?

He didn't seem like a man looking for love, that was certain.

Needing love, maybe. But not looking for it.

Whatever his circumstances, and his reasons, he wasn't inviting anyone into his life, or into his heart. Yet his actions spoke of a lonely man in need of someone to care for. His sad eyes said: I see you, I like you, I want you.

Was that just my own sad, lonely rejected heart filling in the blanks the way I wanted to?

After a while he stomped back upstairs carrying a simple wooden chair with a woven rush seat. The kind that was traditional here in Mexico. He set it down with the back facing me and straddled it, leaning his thick forearms on the back and peering intently at me.

I couldn't help but study his arms. They were impressive, strong and sinuous with muscles, corded veins twisting down his wrists and hands like a river of lava, the deep tan of someone who lived mostly outdoors in the tropics year around, with a dusting of sun-bleached hair. My pulse quickened, and I felt shy under his scrutiny, too shy to raise my gaze to his, too nervous to find out what he wanted.

His arms bore no tattoos but there was one on his chest, previously hidden by his long hair. A twisted wreath of thorns braided with names in script curved over his bulging chest. I couldn't quite make them out but I thought one of them said Megan or Marian. Squinting, I made out blood dripping from the thorns in a way that was both gruesome and heartbreaking. On the other side, and lower, was a circular puckered scar at the base of his ribs, white against his brown skin.

Since he didn't have anything to say I finally looked up, studying his face. He seemed to be forty-ish, his wavy brown hair streaked with gold from the sun, his suntanned face creased on his brow and at the corners of his eyes, and bracketing his full mouth. Not smile lines, more like lines of worry and stress. It was disorienting to look at him, and find him both handsome and sympathetic after our inauspicious encounter earlier today.

"I suppose I should know your name."

"No need." His gaze darted to the side. "You won't be here long. And I doubt we'll meet again."

My heart stuttered at his gruff dismissal. "Nevertheless, it would be civil to make introductions. Since I'm imposing on your hospitality, I would like to have a name to take away to remember this day. My name is Elle."

He grunted again, a short sharp sound that came from low in his throat that seemed habitual. Perhaps that's what came of never having anyone to speak to. "I'd rather you didn't. But you can call me José."

He didn't appear Latino. "You don't look like a José. You're American?"

His brows lifted, and his eyes narrowed as he glared gently at me. I got the impression he might have rolled his eyes if that were his style.

Ignoring my question, he asked, "So. You're on vacation? From the States?"

"Mmhmm. Canada. Visiting my aunt."

"And who's she?"

"Muriel?" I wondered if he'd met any of the other ex-pats in the village, with his anti-social ways. There were only about fifty of them.

He nodded. The way he pushed out his lips in thought snagged my gaze like a marlin on a hook, and I licked my lips, curious about how they would feel. How they would taste. The action drew his attention, but again his gaze flicked away. "The old lady on the hill a few properties back? The writer?"

"Yes, that's her. I'm staying with her for the holidays."

"I've never known her to have house guests before."

So he did know her. "Yes. Well. Just like I did with you I may have imposed myself on her in my hour of need. She's tolerating my presence as long as I don't interfere with her writing."

"That why you were out gallivanting?"

"I wouldn't exactly call it gallivanting. A person has to do something while on vacation. The beach beckoned."

"The beach is the other way, north of the village."

"Too crowded. I was looking for a private place to swim and read."

He huffed with a restrained laugh, not amused. "You found that all right."

I drew a deep breath, filling my lungs, half exasperated and half intrigued. "What's your deal? I know this village is full of eccentric ex-pats, but I got the impression it was a fairly sociable community."

"I suppose it can be, if you're so inclined."

"Have you been ostracized? Or have you got enemies like my aunt?"

His eyes flared with awareness, then calmed. Then his face pulled quizzically. "Your aunt has enemies."

He made this a statement but I gathered he was looking for clarification. I took a breath and let it out. "When I first got off the boat, I only had vague directions to my aunt's house, but I found things got bewildering by the time I got to the village."

"So you asked for directions."

"Yes." I knew I sounded prim and prissy but I was still pissed off that those people could be so mean to a stranger. "Anyway I was given directions to go up the river. They told me she lived there. 'The older Canadian woman.'" I sighed, and watched him quirk one eyebrow up in anticipation of the rest of my story. "I guess everyone was in on the joke. The farther I walked up the river valley, the more people I asked for directions, the more openly everyone laughed at me. It's like a separate tribe up there. Finally someone took pity on me and told me to turn around and take a left at the village icehouse." I pouted. "I was inadvertently made a laughingstock at my aunt's expense. Too bad she didn't care."

"You found your aunt in the end."

"Yes. She explained later that her ex lives up that way, and that apparently some people still resent her for the way that ended."

"I'm not one for gossip, as you might have guessed. You want to fill me in?"

"Well, my aunt moved here over twenty years ago with her lover, and they lived happily together for around ten years. And then she met someone else, and they fell in love. She said she didn't plan it, she wasn't looking for it, but this new woman was her soulmate. Or so she thought."

He tilted his head to the side. "It didn't last."

I shook my head. "The younger woman left after less than a year, and my aunt was heartbroken. I suppose she believes it was just desserts, since she'd discarded her old lover rather abruptly."

"She's been alone ever since."

I nodded, looking at him, pondering his own solitude. "Penance maybe? Or just a broken heart."

He tilted his head again, studying me, his eyes sad and sympathetic, and I wondered why. Then his eyes crinkled at the corners and one edge of his lips curled up. "I'm sorry your intro-duction to the village was so embarrassing. It wasn't your fault."

I huffed out a half-hearted laugh. "I know. I'm used to it. But I felt bad for Muriel. I didn't know her history. She's a bit of an enigma in the family, but I've always admired her independent streak."

"Are you like her? Vacationing alone at Christmas?"

My smile fell. "Not at all. This is my first Christmas away from my whole family."

His face bent in chagrin and he blinked at me, inviting elaboration.

"Actually I'm hiding from Christmas this year." I twisted my lips to the side, flicking my gaze down. "I couldn't face them."

He waited, eyes radiating kindness, and I knew I would get sympathy for my plight.

"I was engaged to be married until a few weeks ago." Lifting my chin, I continued. "Now I'm not. I was dumped."

His mouth pulled down in an exaggerated pout, and he lifted a hand to pinch my chin between his thumb and forefinger. "Poor Elle. His loss."

I huffed again. "Doesn't feel like it."

His small smile was sympathetic.

"Are you … I mean were you … married?" I asked him.

With wary eyes, it took him a long time to decide to answer. When he did, it was with a single word. "Once."

"Do you have kids?"

He jerked back, scowling. "Nosy much?"

"I'm sorry. I only wondered because— " I paused to choose my words more carefully. "The lullaby you were singing. Lavender's Blue. I know it from my work at school. It's an odd song to know unless …"

He stared at me for a long moment, his face folded into a deep, pensive frown. His broad chest moved up and down with his breath, which seemed to quicken. Then he blinked and came back to the moment, saying gruffly. "Not anymore."

"I'm sorry. Divorce?"

His jaw worked as his brow folded further over his eyes, which flashed with unmistakable pain.

He swallowed, lifting his chin. "No." Then, almost as an afterthought he barked, "Enough questions."

"Somebody died," I whispered.

He stopped, closing his eyes, his jaw clenched. Then he nodded, so slightly, almost imperceptibly. But still he nodded, as though he couldn't stop himself from acknowledging them.

I gasped, expecting anything but that. My eyes flooded instantly with tears of sympathy. That explained the air of melancholy that enveloped him. Was this the reason he lived all alone in this remote place, avoiding company?

He pushed back and stood abruptly, but not before I caught the glaze of tears in his eyes. "It was long ago."

It didn't matter how long ago. I whispered, "I can't imagine anything worse than losing your child." Children? I realized he was sensitive, and wounded, and suddenly I wanted to know more about him and why he was here, alone like a hermit.

Pointing at the tattoo on his chest, a symbol of some kind of lost love, I asked. "Is that them?"

Catching my drift, his gaze flicked down to his chest as though he'd forgotten that he'd made a permanent mark there, on his heart. I had the feeling they were not souls that he was likely to forget in any case. "My family." His hand covered the tattoo, slowly caressing down over his sculpted pec, as if it were a substitute for his lost loves. His voice was a whisper, a broken sound, and I suspected his truth was worse than I imagined.

Looking more closely at the tattoo, I realized there were in fact three names inscribed here.

"Your wife died too," I guessed. "Tell me about them?"

His head jerked sharply to the side and back. "No. Look. Here's the situation. I can't leave. And I can't send a message to your aunt. So the best thing is to get you on your feet and send you back. But first I have to talk to you about what you've seen."

"Why can't you go out?" My attention sharpened, suddenly

more alert, equal parts confused and concerned. "What have I seen?"

"This property. This house. Me."

I curled my lip. "Big secret, is it?"

"You have no idea."

I wanted answers, but I couldn't talk anymore. Thinking and crying made my head felt as though it had a hatchet in it and my eyes were heavy with exhaustion. "You wouldn't have pain killers would you?"

"Yeah. Sorry I didn't think to offer it sooner." He got up and went down to the kitchen. A minute later he came back up with a glass of water and handed me a couple of pills. "Acetaminophen. Should help."

He held the pills to my lips and I took them on my tongue, the feel of his warm thick calloused fingers sending a shock of awareness through me. He felt it too. For an instant our gaze flew together like magnets, wary and hot, before I lowered mine. He cleared his throat and set the glass of water to my mouth tilting it carefully so that I could sip and swallow. He did this gently, with the sensitivity that belied his gruff and solitary life, as though once upon a time he had nursed a sick child. My heart broke for him all over again.

As I set my head back on the pillow, my eyes heavy with sleep despite the steady pressure in my head, I realized he had evaded my question. I still knew nothing about him, including I suspected his real name, or why he lived like a paranoid hermit in a tropical jungle and I was never to speak of it.

He left me alone then, and I must have dozed. The sound of him moving quietly around woke me, and I watched him as he carried a light blanket towards the stairs.

"Where will you sleep?"

He turned to me, surprised. "Sorry I woke you. I have a hammock. It's fine."

"Thank you, José," I murmured, drowsy. "If that's really your name."

He paused and stepped to the side of the bed, looking down at me. Suddenly he bent, shocking me by stroking the hair from my forehead and dropped a soft kiss there. "Goodnight, Elle."

Then he left. And instead of falling back to sleep, I lay in the dark thinking about him for a very long time.

Chapter 9

JOE

I WOKE EARLY, as was my habit. I'd lain awake, bothered and confused, half the night. Something about Elle drew me. Was it only that she was the first person I'd spent time with in years? Was I so starved for human contact?

Yes, I concluded. I was. But it was something more. She was easy to be with, especially for someone as prickly as me. She soothed me. She was soft, gentle and infinitely pleasurable to look at. With her angelic light hair and long smooth limbs, her wide innocent warm eyes and her prissy, pouty mouth. My cock twitched and stretched with morning wood that had no where to go. My awareness strayed back to the beautiful woman in my bed. She pulled me in like a siren.

How did she do it? Every conversation we had, I let more and more personal details slip. She disarmed me, and asked just the right questions, in such a way that I felt compelled to reply. Until I stepped away and realized I'd given her enough details to put the pieces together and cause me serious problems. Yet she didn't seem interested in my excuses or evasions. Rather she seemed genuinely interested in me.

The man.

And damn, I craved that like an addict in withdrawal. I wanted to keep her here, forever. I wanted to pull her close, breathe her in, taste her. I was a thirsty, thirsty man.

The way her big brown eyes instantly filled to the brim with tears and spilled over her cheeks like a spring upon learning about my family, nearly undid me. There'd been precious little human comfort and sympathy in the past seven years.

I wondered if Elle's aunt Muriel was the type of woman to panic and call in *la Policia* to search for her adult niece. Somehow I didn't think so, which gave me some comfort that we had a little more time. Though ladylike and refined, and unaccustomed to rustic jungle life, Elle seemed mature and levelheaded. She also appeared to be a woman somewhere in her middle thirties. Given that Muriel was a mature sixty-something independent woman who'd been living alone in this remote village for ten years, and had moved here with her lover twenty years ago, I doubted that she would be prone to hysteria. The safest strategy was to nurse Elle back to health and send her on her way, my secrets hopefully locked away safely behind her discrete, sexy lips.

I had to stop thinking that thought. It was one torture after another. First her soft curves in her prim little blue swimsuit, temptingly female, her round breasts plump as mangoes practically falling out, in my arms, in my bed, though she was granted unconscious. Then her precise and prissy way of moving, and talking like a schoolteacher, her scolding, righteous manner and her sweet pink soft luscious lips. She was no loose party girl and I found her reserve even more compelling. Touching my fingertips, her pink tongue darting out to retrieve the pills nearly sent me into throes of ecstasy.

God help me.

If she didn't leave soon it would take Herculean strength to resist her charms. And I wasn't sure I was up to the task. In fact, I felt myself slipping hour by hour into her gentle sweet net and the thought of her leaving filled me with longing and regret.

I whipped up some *huevos rancheros* and brewed a pot of good strong coffee, and carried it up to the bedroom. I had a crick in my back from trying to sleep in my hammock, which was fine for an afternoon nap, but about as comfortable as a gunny sack for a full night's sleep.

She was still sound asleep, and I set the tray down on the dresser, deliberating whether to wake her. Letting her sleep on and on seemed unwise give the possibility of concussion.

"Elle," I whispered. Nothing. My pulse dashed ahead. A little louder, I hissed, "Elle." Still nothing, dammit. I stepped close to the bed and gently set my hand to her shoulder shaking it.

She jolted upright screaming bloody murder again and struck my chest with her fists until I grab them and held her away. "Lord love a man, stand down woman."

She seemed to come to her senses, her wild eyes clearing from whatever demons haunted her in her sleep. "Oh, oh it's you. I'm sorry I, I—I couldn't remember where I was."

"It's okay. I startled you. I just—wanted to make sure you were doing all right. I brought you some breakfast if you're up for it."

She lay back against the pillows, her fingers rubbing her eyes, kneading her temples. Her hair was tangled, a light web of creases on one rosy cheek, and my chest squeezed, remembering domestic mornings past. My mind played out a future where I woke to a soft, warm woman in my bed, and how lovely that would be. She held her head between her hands like a basketball and scrunched her eyes close tight.

Lifting the tray, I set it on her lap and said, "Does it hurt?"
She sighed. "Yes."
The fact that she chose not to elaborate or make excuses

made me think it hurt a lot, and she didn't have the energy to speak or downplay it. She did however enjoy the eggs with relish, though she moved with care.

"You don't drink coffee?"

Fumbling her fork, she looked at the cup and took another sip. "No, I do. In fact it's delicious but somehow coffee doesn't feel like the thing right now. Maybe..." She waved a hand around her head, and I thought she might be right. In her condition, caffeine might be a bad idea.

"There's more acetaminophen there." She took the pills, washed them down with coffee and set down the mug with a pinched expression.

I grunted, lifting her cup to drink it myself and sat back on the chair as she finished eating. "Feeling well enough to tell me something about yourself?"

She set the tray aside and lay back, closing her eyes. "I talked about myself yesterday. It's you who've been secretive."

"I have my reasons. And as a matter fact yesterday you told me quite a bit about Aunt Muriel, and nothing at all about yourself except your name."

Her lips curled slightly in a smile that acknowledged the truth of my words. "What do you want to know?"

I thought about it. In truth I shouldn't even be curious about her. I shouldn't want to know anything about her except when was she leaving, and could she be trusted with my secrets. Maybe that's why I wanted to know more about her, and her life. At least that's what I told myself.

"Where do you live? What do you do?"

She rubbed her eyes and shook her head, looking up at me with a wry smile. "I live in Vancouver."

Huh. Just north of my former home in Seattle.

"I'm a teaching librarian at a private school."

I smacked the back of the chair with a hoot. "I knew it!"

"Did you indeed?" She gave me the side eye, scrunching her face with a sceptical smirk. "Why did you think so?"

I looked at her, unable to suppress my grin. "I don't know. Something about the way you talk. Maybe wishful thinking. I might have a little thing for schoolmarms."

Her face pinched up, making me laugh. "I feel like I've just been called an pruny old spinster."

"Are you?" I asked, meant to tease, but instead of responding with laughter, or with the righteous outrage that I had hoped to provoke, her face fell. Suddenly her eyes were filled with melancholy and self-doubt.

Her gaze drifted up and out over the treetops to the mouth of the bay where wisps of morning mist hung at the horizon, going a little out of focus as her thoughts wandered far away. "Maybe I am. That's what Austin seemed to think."

"Austin. The fiancé?"

She hummed, her gaze dropping to her entwined hands, and I remembered the things she'd said to me in her delirium, when she'd mistaken me for her ex. I squirmed on the chair, adjusting myself, glad for the shield of the chair's back. Austin was a fool.

"Do you like your work?"

"I love it," she said on a rush of breath. "I love books, am passionate about literacy. And I adore working with the kids so much." She paused, her face flashing in a bright smile. "I'm good at it."

I studied her face, serious and earnest, feeling my face stretch in a reluctant half smile. She was a woman who knew what she wanted, without apology. I admired that. I even thought it would be awfully nice to be one of those things. "I don't doubt it."

A blush bloomed on her cheeks, and her gaze darted away. Adorable. "Hey, can I use the bathroom?"

"Of course." I steadied her arm as she slowly rose from the bed on wobbly legs, relishing any excuse to touch her, walking beside her as she made her way past the screen to the open bath area. When she could lean on the vanity, I stepped away and gave her privacy, dashing to the kitchen to get her a glass of juice.

The water ran, and I heard her soft voice moan. After a few moments of silence, I asked, "Elle? You all right there?"

"I dropped the soap," she mumbled. "Just a little dizzy,"

"You decent?"

"Mhm."

I went back to help her, and after a step she stumbled. I swept her into my arms and strode back to the bed. "I guess that answers the question of whether you're well enough to walk home."

She brought her palm to her face, covering her eyes with a deep sigh. "I'm sorry. I'm sure you want to get rid of me and return to your normal life."

I guffawed, reluctantly setting her down on the bed, my palms sliding over her silken skin. "My life is anything but normal." I resumed my seat at her side, when what I really wanted was to crawl onto the bed and wrap her in my arms again. I handed her the juice.

"Thank you." She sipped, her tongue darting out to lick her lips, and my pulse quickened at the sight. Oh, boy.

"And in case you wondered, there's not much to do most days."

"What do you do?"

I shrugged. "Eat, sleep, work, exercise, read."

"Oh! That reminds me." She pulled a swollen paperback from beside her and showed it to me. "This got wet." Its swollen pages were curled and it fanned open. "Do you think you could put this out in the sun to dry? I'll rip the pages if I try to read it like this."

I took it. "Sure." It occurred to me that she might also enjoy some sunshine, and that it might comfort her and speed her healing. "I could find you something else to read. Would you like to be out in the sun? I can carry you to the terrace."

"That would be nice, if it's no trouble."

I lifted her into my arms, again remembering the way she crooned and caressed me when she mistook me for the idiot Austin. The feel of her soft breasts and bare skin against my chest and stomach sent dangerous fantasies shooting through my horny brain. What the hell was I doing? Together we went downstairs and through my kitchen and living room.

Her eyes went wide as she scanned my space. "Your house is huge."

"By local standards, maybe." A hovel compared to the home I'd left behind in Seattle.

"Did you build it?"

I nodded. "With help, yes."

"Did all this furniture come in by boat?"

"That's the usual way. By barge. But..." I reconsidered telling her about the helicopter pad at the top of my acreage, on the mountain top plateau, where all manner of supplies and gear got dropped off in the middle of the night. Again, I almost let slip more details she didn't need to know.

Her face turned to me, curious, and I kept my gaze averted. "Never mind." I stepped out past the large palapa-roofed main rooms to the upper terrace, partially shaded by a stretch of canvas suspended between trees and poles, hoping to distract her.

She drew in a breath. "Oh, my. This is beautiful," she said. "Look at all the gorgeous trees. Mangos. Papayas. Limes. Avocados." She sighed. "This place makes Muriel's look like a shack, and I thought it was so pretty. This must have cost a fortune way out here."

I grunted. It did, though a pittance in reality for me. I'd been here so long I scarcely noticed the details anymore, the grove of trees merely a source of food. I tried to see it through her eyes. I guess it was impressive, in its way. I carried her to a chaise lounge and set her down. "This okay?"

"Delightful. If I sit still I can pretend I'm at a luxury resort instead of convalescing in the secret lair of a reclusive … a reclusive what? What are you, José? A Hollywood producer? An arms dealer?"

A bark of laughter escaped at her wild guesses. She was closer to the truth than she could possibly know. Though her guesses were playful, her wariness at the truth shone in her big brown eyes.

Reading my expression she asked in a hushed tone, "Are you really a smuggler of contraband?" stilling my laughter.

"No. I'm a businessman, Elle. That's all. One with dangerous enemies." Fuck. Again with the confidences. I think I'm being coy when in fact I'm giving away information that I should just keep to myself. But I couldn't stop myself from talking to her. Idiot! I walked away, back to my main room to scan a few books on the shelf. Many of mine were also weathered from open air living, though Luis made sure I received a fresh supply. Her soggy book was a historical novel, so I picked another WWII story that I thought might interest her and strode back, sitting on a deck chair beside her.

She took the book from my hand, curious, and peered at its cover, immediately interested.

"Have you read it yet?"

She shook her head. "It's quite new. You read a lot?"

"Not much else to do." Another detail I didn't need to reveal was my satellite feed, which allowed me to stream news, and, if I wanted them, shows, to my computer. The truth was I preferred reading. It helped to wile away more time, was portable, and quiet. A man got used to the quiet.

"Do you prefer historical fiction?"

I shrugged, lifting the book I'd been reading. "I like Westerns. Among other things."

"What's your guilty pleasure?" Her voice curled around her smile, and I glanced up, my eyes drawn to her sweet face.

I shook my head, biting back another smile. I couldn't seem to stop them. "I might read a few space operas."

"No thrillers? Murder mysteries? That seems like your kind of thing. Man of mystery and all that."

I sobered. "No. I prefer to be diverted from real life."

She gasped. "I'm so sorry. I didn't think." She paused, frowning at me, her face bent intently. "Were they..." She gasped again, her voice dropping to a whisper, lifting at the end with disbelief as her fingers flew to her lips. "Were they murdered?"

My jaw clenched tight, and I squeezed my eyes tight, dropping my head. "Please stop asking questions."

"I'm sorry. I'm so sorry."

For fucks sake. If she started crying again I was going to have to run up the mountain to the heli pad to pick up the dropped packages just to unleash my emotions somehow. Why was she doing this to me? I felt like my tightly strapped down feelings were leaking out all over the place, like a smashed, fallen coconut.

I sighed, lifting my gaze to meet hers. "It's okay. Don't worry. It was a long, long time ago."

She curled her lips inward, biting down on them as if to physically restrain her curiosity.

Her shoulders leaned awkwardly, and I stood to adjust the cushions behind her.

"Why don't you just settle in and read for a while? I've got an errand to run." As I bent over her, she looked up, and our faces were but inches apart. The scent of her, unmistakably feminine, set my blood racing. I paused, hovering, watching her softly curving breasts rise and fall with her rapid breathing, as my own accelerated. Our gazes met, and I swear the expression in hers was hungry. Did she feel as attracted to me as I was to her? Her lips parted, and a jolt of need slammed through me like a lightning bolt. Holding her gaze, I leaned down and lightly, experimentally, touched my lips to hers.

Oh, why did I do that?

Soft, cool, plump. She gasped softly, then exhaled, her breath tickling my skin, setting it on fire. My cock shot to fully hard in seconds. I pressed closer, testing the corner of her sweet lips with the tip of my tongue, unable to resist the temptation. She whimpered. A moan rose up from my chest and I deepened the kiss, touching her tongue lightly.

She gasped then and I came to myself, pulling away, frowning.

"Sorry. I don't know why I did that."

"Do it again," she whispered, setting her fingertips against my bare chest. And Goddam me, but I couldn't stop myself from taking her up on her offer. The second kiss lasted longer, went deeper, with just a little more tongue, hot and silken. It was so hot, lust shot through every vein and cell in my poor starved body. It was her turn to moan, squirming, and mine to grunt with urgent need. I tore myself away abruptly.

"Enjoy your book. Rest as much as you can so you can go back to Muriel's soon. Christmas is coming."

I needed to run up the mountain. Right now.

***

ELLE

JOSÉ STAYED AWAY A LONG TIME. He took off like a man pursued. And maybe that's how he felt. The sexual tension between us was combustive. And obviously it was mutual.

While he was gone, I lay on the chaise with my eyes closed, dozing a little in the sun as the afternoon wore on. Dreaming about his kisses. Reliving them, detail by delicious detail. They were so hot, I was melting, trembling with want. How could I want him so badly? More than I ever desired Austin, who was quickly fading into a distant memory.

Why was I so powerfully attracted to José? I didn't know anything about him, including his real name. And what I did know wasn't good. He could be a dangerous man. He looked, behaved and lived like one. And even if he wasn't, there was no future here. I shook my head to clear it of the lustful fantasies that had been playing on repeat since he left. It was a terrible idea.

Yet a very compelling one.

Maybe his very mysterious dangerous edge was what I found so sexy. In some ways, it was Austin's risk-taking extreme sports that I found sexy too. I couldn't participate in them the way he wanted me to. But I got a little vicarious thrill every time he raced, flew or jumped.

The longer I lay there thinking about it, the more it made sense to me. Everyone in my family was a successful adventure seeker, fearlessly pursuing their dreams. Except me. Being left behind can make a person yearn for adventure that's forever beyond reach. And yet, growing up, my own meagre attempts at sports or anything active invariably resulted in disaster. Broken things and accidents and humiliation.

Why did I have to be so awkward and clumsy? Why was I so afraid of everything that other people found fun and exciting?

I didn't have the answers. But I was definitely drawn to José.

But maybe that was all I needed. Something - or somebody - to help me get over Austin. A brief fling to make me feel that I'd had an adventure this Christmas, instead of merely hiding from my shame. Then I could go home and start fresh, waste no more time mooning over Austin and my doomed engagement. In fact, I was already there. It was shocking how little I missed him. I felt a stronger pull to José. And a strange sense of affinity. Despite his evasiveness, we could talk. We seemed to have a connection. That was part of the attraction.

I looked up, my daydreams broken by noises.

As if my thoughts had conjured him, José had finally returned. I heard his approach, sandals slapping on the dirt pathway, before he crashed into the house through a side entrance heaving a large box.

His breath was laboured as he set the box down on his table and turned to peer out at me. I lifted a hand in a little wave of greeting.

"Hi. I was beginning to worry that you'd abandoned me here."

He strode out. "Sorry to take so long. I had to pick up a delivery."

His hair was damp from the sweat that coated his brow and the sides of his face and neck. His chest glistened with sweat too, as did his legs, where it ran in rivulets through a fine coating of dust clinging to his leg hair.

"You're filthy. Where did you go?"

He made a sound in his chest, gesturing up. Up the hill behind the house I guessed and wondered who delivered packages up there. But I knew better than to ask.

"You doing okay? Need anything?"

"I'm thirsty. And I wouldn't mind lying down. The sun has made me tired and my head hurts again."

He grunted. "I'm sorry. I shouldn't have left you in the sun without water. Just a sec." He strode into he house and returned a minute later with a tall glass of water, handing it to me.

While I drank, he said, "I'll just have a shower. Then I'll take you in."

"I wouldn't mind a shower myself. I'm over warm now and I'm not feeling very fresh."

His sharp blue eyes pierced me with the intensity of his stare as his chest rose and fell, rose and fell. I stared back. Was he thinking what I was thinking? We could shower together.

"I'll see what I can do. After." His jaw set, he turned away.

I moved to rise. "I can walk myself. I'm sure I can."

He scowled back at me, back to his grouchy self. "Better not attempt it when I'm not here. Just in case you get another dizzy spell."

With my head throbbing again, I couldn't disagree, so I lay waiting for him, feeling discouraged that I would ever have an adventure, either under my own power, or with sexy José, who seemed to have cooled his jets and withdrawn from our sizzling attraction earlier.

Some minutes later he returned, clean and refreshed, his hair washed and wet, wearing plain blue nylon swim shorts. But his wary gaze on me was only slightly cooler, still burning with blue ice, and I realized he was fighting his own attraction.

He hoisted me up and carried me back through the living room, upstairs to the bedroom loft. As we passed, I studied the package on the table. It was a large plastic bin, unmarked. And it was wrapped snuggly in a nylon net, with a loop at the top, as if it had been hoisted up. Or lowered? How strange.

"What did you have delivered?" I probed.

He scowled. "I'll let you know when I open it. Sometimes there are surprises."

Peculiar. I wondered who he had in the outside world that took care of his needs, and sent him things he hadn't asked for.

Instead of carrying me to the bed, he passed right by and took me outside. Past the toilet and sink, around the corner of a curved tiled wall, we stepped into a large outdoor shower, open to the jungle, with a panoramic view of the bay beyond the line of trees that topped the ridge to one side. In this direction, there was no evidence of the village or ex-pats houses that lined the shore and river valley. We could have been anywhere wild and uninhabited. Utterly alone.

He'd set a plastic chair there, in the shower, and set me on it. Then he gently untied the fabric bandage wrapping my head, and peeled away the gauze, leaning over me to study the back of my head. "Looks a little better," he murmured near my ear. "The swelling's gone down, and the wound is closing."

Relieved, I said, "Can I wash my hair now?"

"No time like the present," he said, turning on the water. "It takes awhile for the sun-heated water to make it through the pipes. Might as well take advantage of it."

The water was lukewarm, though still shocking agains my sun heated skin. It was refreshing like no other shower I'd had. My skin tingled, and I ran my hands over my arms and thighs, closing my eyes. He stepped into the spray with me, partially blocking the flow, and I felt his hands lightly on my hair. The scent of shampoo, coconuts and tropical fruit, met my nose as he worked it slowly into my dirty matted strands, massaging a little at a time.

"It'll take a while to get the dried blood out."

"It's okay," I answered, my eyes still closed. "Mmm. It feels so good. I could stay here all day." Contentment washed over me with the water, and I revelled in his gentle attentions as he rubbed and rinsed until my hair felt squeaky clean again. His tenderness made my heart swell with longing. He withdrew his hands.

Thinking we were done, I opened my eyes. "Thank you."

He stood above me, his gaze hot again, and his expression stern. Then he lifted a bar of soap and began to slide it over my arms and my back, moving in small circles as he stepped behind me. I swallowed, realizing he was losing the battle, and my blood heated under his touch. I turned to look at him, water sluicing over his bulging muscles and strong limbs, and caught the tenting in his shorts that he'd tried to hide by moving behind me.

Feeling brave, I walked myself around until I faced him, and lifted my hands to rest them on his ripped abs. He sucked in a breath, moving away, but I cupped my hands around his hips, staying him. I glanced up to his face to see him watching me, unmoving, his lips open, his brow pulled down.

He waited to see what I'd do, but he wouldn't stop me. Not now. So I kept going. I did what I'd fantasized about, running my palms over his sculpted torso, letting my fingers dance over his carved six pack and trace the valleys that pointed down like a runway, to the large bulge in his shorts, which seemed to grow ever larger. Now I couldn't go back. I had to see him. To feel him.

I traced the waistband of his shorts, tucking my fingertips beneath the edge. His hands came up to rest on my shoulders.

"Elle," he choked out. "We shouldn't. I can't."

"Can't what? Feel pleasure?" I smiled.

His head shook slightly, but his eyes begged me to continue, so I did. I pulled, slowly sliding his shorts down over his narrow hips, feeling the tight tendons and hip bones close to the surface. Hard. He was all hard. In the most incredible way. Then I freed him, and his erection sprung free as if leaping out to greet me. He sucked in a breath, and held it, anticipating my next move.

I took him between my hands, holding his impressive girth softly but firmly for a moment, just delighting in the size of him, his masculine beauty, silk and steel. Running my hands up and down his length, pressing slightly, I slid one hand under to cup his sac, and squeezed.

"Hello there," I murmured, bringing my lips to his head, rubbing his wet smooth tip against my lips.

"Oh my fucking ... Gah," he grunted, his stomach clenching as he lifted his hands from my shoulders to span the sides of the tiled shower walls, his arms taut as Samson trying to bring down the palace. Satisfied I had both is attention and consent, I opened my mouth and dragged my tongue up the underside of him, sliding the head between my lips. "Elle," he breathed. "I can't ... I haven't had ... I won't..."

I understood what he was saying. He wouldn't last. He was too sensitive. Too deprived. I pulled him out. "It's okay. This is for you." And then I resumed my licking and sucking, eliciting desperate groans and grunts from him, his hips agreeably pushing forward, until his legs shuddered and I feared he'd collapse. My own arousal had risen to match his, my nipples taut, my centre pulsing with need.

Before that could happen, he pulled away and turned, shooting his load behind me into the shower with a sharp choked cry. That sound I recognized from my first afternoon here, and I realized he'd jerked off in the shower that day. Because of me?

Resting both hands on the wall, he dropped his head between them, panting, his wide shoulders sagging.

I waited. And when he'd recovered, he bent over me, lifting my chin with his fingers, covering my mouth with his own. There was no hesitation this time, his open mouth possessed mine, his tongue diving deep into my mouth in an erotic dance. It was a thank you. But it was more than that. He was saying we weren't finished yet, and my tingling, buzzing core tightened around nothing, hungry for more of him. Hungry to be stretched and filled by him.

"You taste like soap," he said, grunting and turning the shower back on, swiping his hands over my face, my shoulders and arms. Then he dropped his palms over my collar and breastbone, pausing with his palms just above my breasts, and met my gaze. "I haven't touched another person, let alone a beautiful woman, in seven years. Please let me."

I smiled up at him. "Please do."

He knelt in front of me, like a man at an altar, and his palms slipped lower, covering my breasts lightly, feeling their heft and shape. He closed his eyes and said, "I've died. I've died and gone to heaven." Then, opening his eyes, he reach around behind and undid the clasps of my swimsuit top, letting it fall and stared at my breasts for a full minute. "I love your tits so much. They're amazing." And he bent his face toward me and pressed it between them, slowly dragging his cheeks, his chin, his mouth back and forth, his rough beard scratching and tickling, driving me to new heights of need. He licked my skin, laved my hardened nipples, and finally took first one and then the other into his mouth and sucked like an artist. He worshiped my breasts and I relished every moment, my core zinging with ever growing need, praying that he planned to follow through on his implied promises.

At some point, I hardly registered, his talented mouth worked its way down my ribs and stomach, over my thighs, into the creases of my hips. He nudged my knees further apart and tucked his face there, burrowing deeper and deeper, licking the water from my skin, and yet making me wetter and wetter.

He pulled off my swimsuit bottoms and I threw back my head and gave him access to every private corner, and it was worth it. He took his time, getting to know the shape of me, tracing every line with his tongue, sucking and rubbing until I trembled and came apart, shuddering and keening, more uninhibited than I had ever been with Austin. I would have fallen from the chair if José hadn't held me firmly in place, his hands tightly gripping my hips.

Then he shut off the water once more and lifted me, carrying me to the bed. This time, he lay down beside me, big spoon to my little one, and held me tight to his chest, his breathing heavy and slow in my ear, until we both drifted off, though it was still early evening. As I fell asleep, my last thought was, it's just a healthy mutual attraction. A little non-committal sex play. Just letting off steam. And he obviously needed it as much as I did. No expectations. No harm.

ELLE

. . .

WHEN I AWOKE it was dark and José was gone. Lifting myself, I peered into the dim moonlit interior, listening for him. "José?" He wouldn't leave me alone again. Not after what we'd shared.

A flickering light appeared on the stairs, bouncing, and I realized it was a candle. Carrying the candle came José, dry and dressed in new shorts and a t-shirt, the first time I'd ever seen him in a shirt.

"You covered up your beautiful muscles."

He chuckled. "It's a little cooler tonight. Might rain." He set the candle on the dresser that abutted the bed and sat beside me, resting a hand on my hip, and looked down at me.

Then he sighed. "I don't know what the hell we're doing, but … I can't get enough of you. And since you'll be here another day or so, we might as well enjoy it. I guess."

I smiled up at him. "I guess."

He leaned down to kiss me, short and sweetly demanding. "But I don't have any condoms. And I somehow doubt you brought any to the beach the other day."

My smile fell. "No."

We shared a wry smile by candlelight. The downside of being a hermit, I supposed.

"I know you're clean, anyway."

He laughed. "Thoroughly."

"How long have you been here, anyway?"

He sobered. "Six-and-a-half years."

My breath quickened at the thought of all that powerful masculinity bottled up for so long and inexplicably, I just wanted it. Against my nature I wanted the danger and thrill of tapping into that virility and need, condom or not. But he put a quick end to my lustful meanderings.

"It's seven years since…" He left the rest unsaid. "I was in hospital for a while. And then set this up." He waved a hand around him.

"Why were you in hospital?"

He lifted my hand, taking my index finger between his, and, lifting the hem of his shirt, set it against the puckered scar on his ribs. "I was shot. Too. I was shot, too. But I didn't die. Though for a long time I wished I had."

"I'm so sorry. Is that why you hide here? Is there really someone looking for you?"

He shrugged. "He hasn't forgotten me, though he doesn't know where I am. He sends annual reminders to my warehouse in Seattle."

"Reminders?"

His smile was hard. "Christmas presents." He lifted a small box, wrapped in festive paper and tied with a red ribbon, tilting it to and fro to show me with a muffled thunk as its contents shifted. "This year's offering." A quiet rumble of thunder lent gravitas to his words.

I frowned at him. "I don't understand. That came in the big box?"

José set the gift down on the bed and leaned back with his hands gripping his knees, drawing a deep breath. "Every year since the attack, a few days before Christmas, he sends one of these. Like a fool, I open them. Inside I find an object that belonged to one of my kids. Or to my wife. A piece of clothing. A toy. An item of jewellery that I recognize." His sigh shuddered as he let it out, and then he continued.

"We were sailing, for the Christmas holidays. The four of us." He swallowed thickly and went on. "Innocently. Unsuspectingly."

I waited, rapt, for finally he was telling me his story. Thunder cracked again in the distance, bringing with it the unmistakable scent of tropical rain.

"On Christmas Day, they came out of nowhere. Boarded our

yacht and shot us. They shot me first, so … there was that small mercy. I fell overboard, unconscious, so I didn't have to witness them slaughter my family. I guess they assumed I'd died from the gunshot, or drowned."

I covered my trembling mouth with my fingers, crying again at the horrible memory. A memory his nemesis made sure he would never forget. For the first time, I fully grasped the sense of imminent danger that he lived with, this killer with a vendetta hovering at the edges of his life, waiting to pounce. Any villain so vindictive as to inflict this wound and continue to probe it was evil incarnate. And I understood why José felt vulnerable.

"Why does he hate you so much?"

"I inadvertently disrupted a huge shipment of cocaine that he'd hidden in a container of goods that I was importing. I alerted the authorities and the drugs were confiscated and destroyed. I'm assuming he suffered significant consequences and is set on revenge."

Sitting up, I wrapped my arms around him, setting my cheek against his shoulder. We sat for a moment in silence, then he kissed the top of my head. "Shall we see what this year brings?"

"Do you really want me to … to …?"

"It's better than being alone, sweetheart. That's for sure." He picked up the gift and began to pull off the wrapping, and I held my breath.

When he opened the box, we both leaned in to peer inside, our breath mingling. I felt heat emanating off of his side, pressed against my hip. I didn't want to see it. I didn't want to know. But I imagined my trepidation was a mere fraction of his own. "What is it?" I whispered.

He barked with bitter laughter. "The fucking bastard." José lifted up the contents for me to see.

I gasped, covering my mouth. It was a rusty black hand gun.

I looked up at him, blinking, confused.

"This was … fuck! Juan Carlos you fucker!" He slammed it

down on the dresser and rose, walking away without another word.

I sat up slowly, staring at the gun, puzzled and a little frightened as, simmering with repressed anger, José stomped downstairs. It was silent afterwards for a long time except for the sound of rain falling on the palapa roof, and I lay still, wondering and worrying about him until the rain lulled me to sleep.

JOE

IT GOT VERY QUIET AGAIN, except for the soft steady sound of the rain, and I realized the last day had been quite different from what I'd become accustomed to. Quiet was the norm, but now, aware of her lying up there on my bed, I tiptoed up and listened to her breathing, at least, and that seemed to change everything. She'd fallen asleep, and I lifted the godforsaken gun and slipped back downstairs.

Filled with pent up frustration over the gun and all that it represented, I'd done what I usually did this time of year. I pulled out my bottle of tequila and settled in at my kitchen table for a long slow slide into oblivion, the fateful Sig Sauer on the table in front of me.

This time of year I couldn't help but think about the past. Of course my thoughts were on Lainie and the kids. But, as I'm sure Juan Carlos's evil mind designed, I tended to dwell on that final cruise, reliving every second, remembering details, who knows maybe even making up a few in my efforts to hold on. Mostly I thought about what I did wrong. What I might have done differently. What different choices I might have made to avoid calamity.

But though I wished my family alive and safe again, there

wasn't much I could think of. I conducted my import-export business carefully, legally and ethically. I was careful who I hired, who I signed contracts with. I inspected farms and factories personally ensuring ethical and sustainable practices. But there was no way to run a business without trusting people. And somewhere along the line I'd put my trust in the wrong person.

But again when I discovered the problem, I didn't hesitate. I called the authorities and exposed the smuggled goods doing everything above board and by the book. I did the right thing. Always.

Hedging out of fear of retribution wasn't even on the table. I didn't do business with criminals or corrupt politicians, so I didn't even think about it.

I sighed heavily and refilled my glass, beginning to feel the welcome numbing effects of the liquor.

Picking up the Sig Sauer, turning it this way and that, examining it, I felt the heft of it in my grip. Then I took it apart to clean it and check the interior and was surprised to find it oiled and clean, as if someone had been using it regularly. It even had a half-used cartridge in it already. I frowned. Was he even aware? Or was he tempting me to do something reckless and desperate with it?

I remembered the feel of it in my hand that fateful day seven years ago. My hand shaking as I held it up, the feel of it slipping from my grip onto the deck when I was shot. My last thought before I stumbled overboard, my last thought in that moment when my family were still alive, not even then knowing what would happen next, was: why hadn't I used it?

I thought I'd done what I needed to do to protect and care for everyone. My business associates, my employees, my clients and of course my family. But still I'd found myself in an untenable situation.

The only thing my mind circled back to time and again was that first few minutes on the yacht. Or before that, when I'd locked up the Sig Sauer out of an excess of caution when the boat charter agent made a point of leaving it for me. Had I been naive about the potential dangers of Americans cruising in the Caribbean? Had I become complacent in my sense of power and control?

In any case, I'd locked up the gun. Retrieving it had wasted precious minutes once Juan Carlos found us and pulled up alongside our boat. But the moment that weighed heaviest on my mind was my hesitation around the use of the gun. If I'd left it locked up, would they have shot us anyway? Or devised some other, less fatal, torment? Did they shoot me because I pointed it first, and kill my family because they were eye witnesses to what they'd assumed was my murder? If I'd actually fired the gun, would it have changed the outcome?

No one could know the answers to these speculations, least of all me.

But the arrival of the gun today was a twist of the knife in a way no previous parcel had been. They had been reminders of my losses, and sent me into spirals of grief. This was different. This was about me, my choices, my failings.

All of it, including the unexpected arrival of my house guest, forced the questions currently on my mind.

Would I make the same choice again, knowing what I knew now? If I ever encountered Juan Carlos again, what would I do? If I had the chance to kill him in retribution, would I? Could I? Would I take the ultimate revenge? And if I were angry enough to do that, who was I? I didn't know myself anymore.

Was I really hiding out here, avoiding Christmas and avoiding life to protect everyone else from further danger? Was I hiding from the possibility of ever caring for anyone again? Or was I simply a coward?

ELLE

IN THE MORNING, he appeared again with a tray of eggs, tortillas and coffee as though nothing had happened. My appetite had blossomed overnight, since we'd skipped dinner, and my stomach growled in anticipation. I sat up carefully, eager to eat as he set the food beside me.

Tentatively, I glanced up, assessing his mood. It seemed to have lifted, washed clean by the overnight storm along with the dust from the palm trees, and the stuffy heat.

"I'm all right," he murmured, sensing my question. His puffy, bloodshot eyes belied his answer. He'd clearly had a terrible night and slept little. He deflected. "How's your head?"

"A little better, I think." He leaned in and fluffed my pillows, propping me up. Then breakfast stole my attention for a while, and he sat beside me, drinking coffee in broody silence.

I felt a little awkward after yesterday. So much had changed in one afternoon. We were still strangers, and yet now we were intimate too. We knew things about each other. We knew each other's bodies. I shivered, remembering our steamy shower, wanting more of that. Yet his mood remained subdued.

Sneaking glances at his face when I could, I knew I had the power to soothe him and distract him. But we needed to move past this barricade. I had never even seen a hand gun except in the movies. "What did that mean? The gun?"

His gaze flicked to the ceiling as he filled his lungs and let out a long, tired sigh. "It's an old Sig Sauer P220. I recognize it from the boat."

I drew in a breath. "Did they use it to …?" I bit my lip, unable to use the words.

José smashed his lips into a tight line, then bit out his answer in a cold monotone. "No. I … when we chartered the yacht, I was told it was there, in a drawer, in case we needed it."

He shook his head. "I'm not, have never been a gun user. I didn't own one. And I didn't like the idea of having it on board with my kids." He bent his head, rubbing his forehead. "I took it from the drawer and put it in a tool box in the engine compartment, locked it up. I figured, it'd be there if needed, but nobody would stumble on it and have an accident. And hopefully I could forget about it." He sighed heavily, his shoulders slumping.

"When Juan Carlos and his thugs chased us down and boarded us, I knew we were in danger. I just didn't understand how much. I sent Lainie and the kids below, but…" He squeezed his eyes tightly shut as if pushing unwanted images away. "Juan Carlos sent his thugs down to grab them. I tried to reason with them, more fool me, but they were brutish, shoving everyone around and screaming at us. He slapped Lainie for talking back, and dragged her up on deck. Then I went for the gun."

"Did you shoot at them?"

José shook his head. "I didn't know if they were planning on taking me, kidnapping my wife, or what. I chased them up, shouting at them, pointing the gun at them like a madman. But I just couldn't shoot. At a human being. I just couldn't do it."

"How many were they?"

"Four. So yeah … I guess it wouldn't have changed the outcome even if I'd made a wild shot at one of them. But I think, maybe that's why they started shooting."

"They shot you first."

He nodded. "I fell overboard, unconscious. That's all I know. Maybe they kept shooting to eliminate witnesses."

I twisted my lips to the side, thinking. "I don't believe, if they were capable of killing your innocent family, your children, in cold blood, that you waving a gun at them would have made the difference."

José raked a hand through his hair. "Maybe you're right, but he knew what I'd feel when I saw this again. It's like he held on to it, waiting for the right moment to torment me with the memories."

I nodded. There was nothing more to say, so I wrapped my arms around him and dropped my forehead to his broad shoulder, just holding on to him.

"If you know who did this, can't the authorities arrest him?"

José scoffed. "They tried. Can't find him. He's even better at hiding than I am."

"I'm so sorry you're trapped in this in-between place, and can't move on."

He shrugged and picked up the tray, carrying it down the stairs. Opposite of the furious, terrifying beast of a man that I'd first encountered, I saw a man defeated.

José returned with the big box in his arms. "I need cheering up. Let's see what other surprises Luis sent me." I scooted back to make room and he pushed the box further onto the bed, opening the lid flaps.

Inside, each item wrapped separately to keep it safe, we discovered food items, some of it luxurious and imported, bottles of fine wine and tequila, a stack of new clothing— basically shorts and t-shirts. He tossed it aside, laughing. "I barely use the clothing. Hold on, what's this?" He unfolded an item and held it up, then burst into laughter. "I assume this is meant for you."

It was a sundress. A pretty sleeveless dress with a square neck, made from a soft cotton printed with brightly coloured papayas and bananas. My gaze shot to José's. "He knows I'm here?"

"Apparently my head of operations and security is all knowing."

Nibbling a fingertip, I asked, "Is that bad?"

He shook his head. "He's trustworthy. The only one who knows where I am." I raised my brows and he added, "Except you. But like my neighbours, you don't really know who I am. Luis is my link to the outside world."

I sat up on my heels, lifting the dress. "It would be nice to wear something besides my swimsuit for a change."

"Let me help." He eased the dress over my bandaged head, and I straightened it over myself.

"It fits fine."

"It's pretty. You're very pretty."

I looked up, returning his smile, glad he was distracted from what I supposed would be a melancholy day. "What else did you get?"

He returned to the box, opening several smaller containers to reveal toiletries, cleaning supplies, batteries, and other mundane household items. He lifted a smaller gift-wrapped box with a card tucked under the ribbon. *"Merry Christmas, Boss,"* I read over his shoulder.

"That's sweet. He must be a very loyal employee."

"He is," José said, thoughtfully, unwrapping the present, obviously curious. "And a good friend. But he doesn't normally send me gift—" He threw back his head and burst into laughter. "Merry Christmas, indeed!" He pulled back the paper to show me an extra large sized box of condoms.

ELLE

THAT WAS the end of unpacking, unless you count me as another box to be explored. José's attention immediately shifted from the box, its contents, its perverse reminder of tragedies past, and Christmas itself. His focus was entirely on me, and the new possibilities his box of condoms opened up.

He set the box on the floor and crawled onto the bed, hovering over me with his big biceps bulging, smirking playfully. "I'm afraid, my dear, that your new dress must be removed."

I let him peel it off of me, along with my swimsuit, tossing all items of clothing aside including his own. It was exquisitely delicious to finally be naked, seeing all of his amazing body, brushing skin to skin as he dragged his mouth over me. We'd crossed a boundary in the shower. There was no more shyness. No more reserve. We wanted each other, and now there was nothing in the way.

"Be gentle with me," he murmured against my neck. "I'm still a very fragile, lonely guy who hasn't had sex in seven years."

Greedily, I ran my hands over his bulging, firm shoulders, pecs, sides and rock hard ass, unable to touch as much of him as I wanted to. "I may have had sex more recently," I rebutted, "but I haven't had this." I bit his shoulder, trying to convey how desperately I was attracted to him. I felt like an animal in heat, crazy with wanting.

"You'd better take it easy, miss," he murmured, dropping a line of kisses along my jawbone. "Lie back and let me do the work. We wouldn't want you to hurt your head. I suspect the orgasms I'm about to give you will be stressful for your compromised health."

Oh-la-la. I relaxed onto the pillow. He was right. I trusted him. He'd deliver, as if this could be anything but mind blowing. I was so aroused all he had to do was look intently into my eyes and I was sure I'd come.

But, thankfully, it took more than that, because he took his time, and was thorough, and I relished every touch. Every kiss, lick, suck and bite that he rendered drove me further towards frenzy. And he was patient and relentless, covering every spot. If I had an erogenous zone, I'm sure he found it, and then some. He gave me so many orgasms that the aftershock of one blurred into the next until I was a quivering mass.

Finally, he rose up onto his knees, flanking my thighs, his massive erection jutting proudly towards me, and handed me one of his precious condoms like a kid on Christmas morning, grinning. I tore the wrapper with my teeth, extracting it and rolling it slowly over his length.

Then José, who was not José, a dangerous man who wasn't, lowered himself over me, nudging my legs apart as he slowly, exquisitely pushed inside me, raising the bar, taking me to new previously unexplored heights, changing my life forever.

Chapter 10

MY MIND WAS MUSH.

Was sex always this amazing? Or had I just pushed the possibility of ever having it again so far from my mind that I'd forgotten?

I just didn't know. But Elle had awakened in me the ability to feel, to desire, to hunger.

After I came to my senses, and Elle stopped quivering and trembling around me with aftershocks, I slowly lowered myself beside her, pulling her close into my arms. I set my head on the pillow, breathing heavily, staring at her profile. Her eyes were open and staring at the ceiling. She seemed to be in as much a state of shock and wonder as I was.

"You're tickling me," she said, and let out a high girlish giggle, wiggling and hunching her shoulder in lieu of scratching the itch, since her arms were pinned in my embrace.

"Sorry," I growled, clearing my throat at the cracked sound

of my voice, kissing her neck, nuzzling her with my beard. "You okay?"

She let out a long sing-song hum, shaking her head from side to side slightly. "Never better." She turned her head to gaze at me, her warm brown eyes dancing over my features. "That was impressive for a man so out of practice, José."

I smiled. Letting her continue to call me that felt absurd. "Joe," I whispered. "Call me Joe."

Her expression opened in mild surprise. "Oh. Look at me. Learning a secret."

"Huh. You've got quite a few, in truth. More than I should have shared." My smile fell. "I've … I've let down my guard more than you know. It's not wise. It's dangerous for both of us."

Lifting a soft, limp hand she lay it along my cheek and jaw. "I won't tell anyone anything. Joe." She whispered my name, trying it on for size. "Your secrets are safe with me."

Though it was a tremendous leap of faith, and I knew nothing about her, really, I still felt in my heart it was true. I could trust her. As if reading my thoughts, she lifted her head, stretching her neck to press her soft lips against mine. Somewhat restored, I hitched up on one elbow and lowered myself over her, covering her sweet mouth with mine, kissing her properly. We luxuriated in the kiss, lazily exploring and caressing each other with our lips, our tongues, nipping with our teeth in languorous post-coital bliss.

Falling back again, I tucked my hands beneath my head, joining her in gazing mindlessly at the gauzy mosquito net canopy separating us from the spiders and scorpions that sometimes dropped from the palapa roof.

"Do you miss your fiancé?"

"What?" I felt her tense at my blunt question, then relax again, her limbs going soft. "You know. I don't, actually. I was just thinking about Austin when you went to get your package yesterday, and I realized I've hardly thought of him. And strangely, though we were together four years, I don't miss him particularly. I feel almost guilty about it."

"Doesn't sound like your heart is broken."

"No. Maybe not. Perhaps my ego. I'm more… disappointed. I thought we were heading in a particular direction. I thought I was finally…"

She stopped abruptly, her head turning away, as if her own thoughts surprised her.

"Tell me," I urged, but let her take her time coming back to me.

She faced up again and in profile, I watched her pink lips purse in rueful thought. "I guess I thought I was finally accomplishing something I'd dreamt of most of my life. That I was about to cross some mysterious boundary into the complete life I'd imagined for so long."

"And what was … is … that dream?"

She scoffed softly. "Nothing so very remarkable. I've never had grand ambitions. Only satisfying work, a home, and someone to love, to call my own. And if it's not too late for me, a little family to grow."

I bit down on the sudden pinch of pain her words caused in my chest, in my throat. On what I had had, and what I had lost. But I said nothing, waiting for her to go on.

"Just a simple, normal, happy life. No wild adventures." She sniffled, dropping her gaze to the rumpled bedding, lost in her thoughts. I set my fingertips lightly on her arm, compelled to connect, to comfort her. At least to let her know I understood.

Glancing up, she continued. "Now I realize I held on too tightly to Austin when we weren't right for each other. My window of opportunity is closing. Maybe if I'd let go sooner I might have found the right partner to make my dreams come true before it's too late."

I stayed silent thinking about my broken life. Where would we all be now, my perfect little family, if I still had them? Would

I be spending long days at the office, flying up and down, making deals, running my business and ignoring them the way I had? Would I be scrambling to take a break from the demands of my business to spend a few days at Christmas with them?

"What about you? What is your dream?" she asked.

I rolled to my side, propping my head on my arm to see her better. "Hmm. I haven't dared to dream for a long time. Not even to imagine a return to some semblance of my former life. It doesn't feel real. Or possible. And it doesn't even feel right. Like I don't deserve it."

"Why? It's not your fault you were targeted by criminals?"

"Isn't it?

Elle sat up suddenly. "No! Of course not." Her face twisted wryly, one corner of her mouth pulling in as she tilted her head, studying me. "You weren't involved in smuggling drugs. You stopped them. It's not your fault they chose to be criminals, or even that they were violent and vengeful. You're not, Joe."

I covered her hip with my hand, squeezing, silently thanking her for her words of comfort and kindness. Not that it relieved my guilt and sense of responsibility for my family's deaths. She didn't know. "I am though," I whispered. "A man is always responsible for his family. I put them at risk. I failed to protect them."

She took my face between her palms, bringing her forehead to lightly touch mine, closing her eyes. "Joe. Oh, Joe. Don't think that way. You deserve to be happy too. You can't carry this the rest of your life."

What was she trying to tell me? Was she only feeling sorry for me? Or was she imagining that we could have a future. That I might factor in some way into her dreams if I could make room in mine. I clenched my teeth, worrying the inside of my cheek. I hoped not. However sweet that fantasy might be for a brief moment, it wasn't possible.

She sank back onto the bed, letting one palm slide softly over my shoulder, across my chest. She tapped my tattoo, reading. "Megan. Lainie. Max. Which one is your wife?"

My throat closed up, burning. I hadn't said her name aloud in years. Drawing a shaking breath, I whispered, "Lainie," as if calling her name out would raise her ghost from the depths of the sea.

Elle pulled her lips between her teeth for a moment, blinking. "And Megan was the eldest? Your daughter?"

I nodded, swallowing the salt of tears that pooled in the back of my throat.

"And Max. The smallest."

"Nine." My voice emerged garbled. Drowned. I swallowed and swallowed again, licking the salty tear that tracked down my cheek to my lip, cooling.

Elle leaned in and kissed the tears from my lips, my cheeks and chin, wiping the rest away with her palms.

"What do you wish for now?"

"Everything I wish for is in the past, Elle. I wish I'd worked less. Been less self-absorbed. Appreciated my family more. Played more. Laughed more. Spent just a little more time and effort showing them I loved them. Precious irreplaceable time."

Elle laced her arm around me, under mine, and I pulled her close, seeking comfort and human warmth. Something I'd craved without realizing how much I'd missed it. I tucked her head beneath my chin, enjoying the small, delicate feel of her next to me. The fit, so good. Some minutes passed in silence, each of us lost in our own thoughts. Our own regrets.

After a moment, the tightness in my chest eased a little, and I drew a breath and let it out on a sigh.

Eager to move beyond my melancholy, I caressed her back and said, "What about your family made it feel safer to come here to stay with your eccentric old aunt than go home? Wouldn't they have … I don't know … commiserated with you?"

"Oh, yes. In their way, I suppose."

I stroked her neck and the underside of her chin with one fingertip, lifting her face to meet her gaze, questioning.

She blinked and tipped her head to the side. "It's hard to explain how small they make me feel, how much I feel like a misfit. An outcast. Even though I love my family, and I know they love me, I still feel like an outsider."

"I think some people always feel that way. Maybe you're just more…" I hitched a shoulder, searching. "More self-conscious, or more contemplative?"

"Mmm. That doesn't explain the fact that I really couldn't, I don't know, participate fully in all the things."

"Things?"

She tsked. "Games, sports, outings. Everything I tried was a disaster. I held everyone back. I had accidents. Made messes. I'm awkward, clumsy, slow. It's all true. And people got tired of waiting for me. I got tired of everyone waiting, laughing at me and pitying me. It was easier to let them go and stay behind. Until that's just what I did."

"So your talents aren't physical. Except of course…" I let my words trail off, stroking her shoulder, the side of her beautiful, round breast, the soft skin of her ribs and hip, smiling. "I'd say you definitely have talents. Perhaps just those your family don't appreciate."

"Well, that's true. Yet I never got over wanting to be accepted and included. To be admired like the others."

"I have nothing but admiration for you." I dropped a soft kiss on her forehead.

She smiled wryly, appreciating my gesture, yet I could tell it didn't quite console her. She still believed she was faulty somehow.

"Tell me about some of them. Who's so accomplished compared to you?"

She shook her head. "Oh, all of them. My sister Delia, for example, is a successful dentist and she scuba dives. My brother

James can do no wrong. He's a talented musician, plays in a jazz quartette, has a degree in music history, teaching at university and a super successful podcast."

"That is impressive. Who else?"

"My best friend Laura. She has a thriving interiors company, a handsome, successful fiancé."

I kept my face serious as she went on. "And?"

"My younger cousin, Tannis." Elle pushed herself up to sitting, warming to her subject, and it seemed to me she was in the habit of enumerating the successes of the people in her life, and making herself feel small in comparison. "She's eight years younger than I am, and yet ten times as able. She's a straight A student studying law, is on the varsity track team and runs like the wind, skiis exceptionally well, plays the cello and the flute superbly. She's active in student body politics, charities and clubs. And before you conclude that she's a nerdy try-hard, she's also tall, slender, beautiful, graceful and very popular with everyone she meets."

I let out a slow whistle. "I don't know anyone who'd measure up to that. But I do wonder if a person that's stretched that thin can be happy. Does she ever just chill?"

"It's true her life is extremely programmed and she's intense and driven. But, the point is, she's just so good at everything she tries. The best. She's perfect. And I don't envy her or resent her in the slightest. I love her. I just can't help feeling like an awkward ugly duckling next to her, and wonder how I ended up so hopeless."

I gently pulled her down again and wrapped my arms around her. "You're no ugly duckling, that's the truth. You're the most beautiful woman I've ever had the chance to know."

She fell quiet for a long moment. "What about your wife?"

I took a minute to consider my answer. "Lainie was… she was a very attractive woman, very smart and kind. A great mom. I loved that she was competent and caring. Looking back, I think… I loved her because we fit together so well. We were good life partners. But I don't remember ever feeling the sort of … wonder I feel when I look at you."

"Wonder?" Her tone was skeptical.

"Mhm. When I look at you," I tightened my grip on her, "Touch you, taste you, I feel a little bit like I've been drugged. Like someone's sprinkled fairy dust all around. It kind of stops me in my tracks and I forget my thoughts."

She laughed, a sweet, tinkling laugh like honey and chimes, and I added one more thing about Elle that bewitched me.

"That's it," I added. "You've bewitched me, enchanted me. That's something I've never felt before."

She hummed and leaned into me, and for a moment we lay together, holding on, listening to the sound of our own breathing and the birds chattering in the forest. I never wanted to let go of this, to let go of her. I could wish to be the man who made all her dreams come true. To devote myself to her well-being, her pleasure. Be the one to remind her daily of her special qualities and talents. And her security.

And that thought doused me with ice cold reality. I could never be the man to give her the happily ever after she wanted and deserved. Except for this moment, and this moment only. Damned if I didn't like her a lot. She soothed and melted my scarred heart and she turned me on something fierce.

She looked up and met my gaze, and I held hers, held her for a moment, just soaking her in. The earth seemed to shift under us, and I knew, if life had dealt me a different hand, I could love this woman. I could love her so hard. Unbidden, the thought formed in my head: And this time I would do it right.

But that was not my reality. Whatever this was, whatever was happening, it was for here and now. I could and I would enjoy every moment of it. But what happened in Yelapa stayed in Yelapa. And then we would part and go our separate ways.

Chapter 11

ELLE

THE WAY JOE looked at me. It filled me with such warm and fluttery feelings that I had never experienced before. He saw me, and knew me, and accepted me. There was no hint of reproach or pity in his sparkling blue gaze. If he smiled, it shone with delight. I felt seen and admired, and my chest filled up with joy like a helium balloon. I was afloat.

I felt much better this afternoon. I could stand and could walk steadily without my head swimming and throbbing with pain. Tomorrow was Christmas. I had to return to Muriel's and let her know I was all right. Surely if I didn't come back for the holiday she'd begin to worry, if she hadn't already.

But I didn't want to leave Joe.

After Joe cleared away the breakfast dishes, he helped me walk down to the terrace, and we both stretched out in the sun to read. He brought us iced hibiscus tea and quesadillas, and seemed for the first time to relax.

He sat at my side and fed me quesadillas, laughing when

melted cheese dribbled down my chin. "Having a little trouble there?"

"I told you I'm clumsy." I lifted the heel of my hand to wipe my chin, and he took my wrist and pulled it away.

Leaning in, he licked me clean, teasing with kisses on my ear and neck and shoulder until I giggled.

"I haven't noticed that you're especially clumsy, sweetheart. Just a bit too self-conscious, maybe." With a fingertip under my chin, he raised my face and planted a greasy kiss on my mouth. "Mm-Mm."

If I let myself, I could easily imagine we were a couple vacationing at an exclusive resort in Mexico. The harsh truth of our circumstances, hiding behind the sweet flickering illusion of normalcy, could for the moment be swept behind a curtain of make believe, like the harsh light of day and its burden of responsibility is momentarily forgotten in the darkness of a matinée movie theatre.

The afternoon dissolved in comfort and ease as we talked about our favourite books and authors, the places we'd travelled, our favourite foods and music. Our tastes were not in perfect alignment, but there was plenty of overlap, and just enough differences to make for spirited debate and teasing.

When a digital alarm trilled, the interruption felt jarring, breaking the magical spell.

"You all right out here for a bit?" he asked, setting his book down. "That'll be Luis checking in. I have to take the call or he'll worry."

"Of course. Take your time." I put a finger in my book and set my head back, closing my eyes to rest as Joe stepped into the house and sat at his desk.

Joe took a long time, the muffled sound of male voices volleying for many minutes, and when he returned, he seemed preoccupied. Worried about something.

"Everything okay?" I asked.

"Sure. Yeah. Just business. There's always something to respond to. Some decisions to make." He sunk back onto his lounger beside mine, but didn't resume reading and seemed to fidget, his pensive gaze on the trees as he worked his jaw.

"I'll have to head back soon," I said, wistfully.

He nodded.

"I'm so hot now. Wouldn't it be lovely to take a dip in the ocean?"

Joe blinked, turning to face me with a tight smile. "I don't go down to the beach."

"Never? You've really never left the property since you got here? Not even to sneak down to the ocean for a swim. Please, can't we?"

He shook his head. "Never. Not safe for me to be seen. Not safe to let my guard down."

"That's tragic. To live in this beautiful tropical paradise, above your own perfect slice of white sand beach, completely private, and never set foot on it? It breaks my heart."

His shoulder twitched. "*Que sera.* And no place is private anymore, with electronic surveillance and satellites. It's much harder to disappear than you might imagine."

His complete resignation to his reclusive lifestyle left my gut unsettled, twisting and tight. This was so wrong. After all that he'd lost, that he should pay with his freedom for the wrongdoing of others. No matter that he felt guilty, that he felt responsible for his family's tragedy, he really was the innocent victim. I fervently wished there was some way to free him from this prison.

A while later, we heard the low *whump-whump-whump* of helicopter blades in the distance. Joe stood up, alert. "I'm sorry to leave you again. I've got to head up the mountain. Do you want to go inside?"

I peered up at him, certain he was stressed about something. I worried that my being here was causing problems for him, but he hadn't said so. "No. I'm fine. And I can walk if I need to. My head's much steadier."

He hesitated, studying me with a serious expression, his eyes sparkling, then nodded sharply and spun on his heel, heading up the dirt path to the south of the house.

It wasn't yet sunset, but the sun had sunk lower in the sky, casting long fingered shadows across the terrace. I waited a while longer, but Joe took forever and I grew restless. I'd thought about waiting to go back to Muriel's until morning, but it felt wrong. I'd been away long enough, and no matter what Muriel said she wanted, I'd planned on spending Christmas Day with her. She was family, after all. There were things I wanted to do before the party in the afternoon.

I stood up and walked inside, glancing around. I had little to gather that was mine, but I slipped on the sundress, gathered my ruined book, sunglasses and towel and tucked them into my bag, preparing to leave. If Joe could walk with me down the path, we could say our good-byes and perhaps I could have a short swim alone before walking back. Turning, I squinted out over the tree tops to the shoreline across the bay and confirmed what I already knew. The tide was on its way out, already quite low. My window to leave approached.

"Joe, where are you?" I mumbled.

I stepped to the path and peered upward, but could see nothing but a trail disappearing into dense foliage and trees. Was he okay? Following him up there felt like an intrusion, and judging by how long it took and how dirty and sweaty he'd been upon returning last time, not something I would wish to attempt. Was it Luis he'd gone to meet? Or was something wrong? My pulse accelerated as my mind spun through different scenarios. Could he be injured? In danger?

Damn it. I had to leave. Surely he must know that this was it. I had to return this evening. But I couldn't leave without saying good-bye. That felt wrong. Unless … Is that what he wanted? Did he want me to disappear to avoid any awkwardness?

Unbidden, a lifetime of rejection flooded over me in a montage of memories. My skin seemed to shrink, my stomach falling with the realization that this momentary dalliance with Joe was just a dream. It wasn't real. I was still the awkward misfit. Always left behind, sent away, excluded. Abandoned. Austin breaking off our engagement was simply the last in a long line of rejection. Something about me caused people to cast me off, unwanted.

I stood for a few minutes considering this possibility. That didn't seem like Joe. We'd got to know each other. It didn't sit right with me, and yet we both knew this interlude was ending. We may not have a future, but we had shared this time, he'd saved me and cared for me. It wasn't right.

Was I being naïve? Idealistic? Nevertheless, this time I wouldn't be the one rejected. I'd be the one to walk away.

I released a frustrated sigh. Come on!

The minutes ticked on as I paced around his house and terrace, stopping to listen intently for any sound of his return. The light changed, turning from white to shimmering gold to pink, and I knew I was running out of time. Both low tide and sunset would happen soon, somewhere around six to six-thirty. If I slipped through, I'd have just enough light to head back safely. Why wasn't he back?

Frustrated, I hunted for a piece of paper to write him a note. Finding none, I tore the blank flyleaf from my wrinkled paperback and rummaged around his computer desk, finding a blunt pencil. The veil had fallen, the illusion was over. I wrote:

Dearest Joe,

I hope you're okay. I'm out of time and worried about getting back along the path this evening. I'm going to head down now. I'll wait on the beach until the rising tide decides for me when I must go. I hope to see you, to say good-bye. To thank you. I wish you a Happy Christmas, if possible. I won't forget you.

xo, Elle

Okay, it was time. The electric fence was a problem, though. I searched his house for an obvious electrical panel but again, struck out. How was I to do this? Could I get across without shocking myself? I picked up the sturdy plastic box his shipment had come in and set it on the floor, testing to see if it would bear my weight. It seemed okay so I took it with me.

The wide open terrace where we'd spent our cozy afternoon gave way to steps, and a series of lower terraces, one after another. I'd seen none of this, since I'd been unconscious when he'd carried me up. Then I came to the narrow section of path and wove my way through the trees and dense foliage, eventually coming to the high rock step. This I recognized, and glancing around, I saw where Joe had repaired the breached fence. The broken tree lay on the ground nearby and I stopped to think.

It would have been so much better to cut power to the fence, but there was no time now to figure out how. And tossing the tree across the fence would break it again. I didn't want to do that and make work for him. My plan to climb and try to leap over was my only hope.

If I set the box on this side, and lifted the branch over, perhaps I could create a bridge to the other side. Joe would find the box and take it away. Assessing the slope of the land, and the arrangement of rocks, I picked my spot and set the box against a wooden pole. Then I dragged the surprisingly heavy branch along, climbed onto the box and lifted the branch, carefully propping it against the pole. I stepped back considering this arrangement. It was precarious at best. If I screwed it up, I'd fall on the other side, but at least I'd be over. Hopefully I didn't land on a rock this time, but I'd be prepared. Worst case scenario, I'd get electrocuted, but I wouldn't die of it. Right?

As I wrestled with the tree, lifting it with shaking arms to the other side, careful not to touch the electrified cross wires, balancing a notch against the pole and checking it for strength, I thought of Joe.

I was so sad to leave him.

He was attractive as sin. Kind and smart and funny. I liked him so very much, but he was exactly the opposite of what I needed. He was dangerous, worse than Austin was, a loner, and couldn't give me what I wanted. Stability, a home and a family. I couldn't risk losing my heart to such a man. Even if on some level I knew I already had.

Miraculously, I was able to balance on the pole and tree with my bare feet, holding my body still and steady until I was past the wires and could clamber down the other side. It was not elegant, but I'd done it.

Standing on the other side of this barrier felt finite. Joe lived on the other side, alone. And here I was. Apart.

My face flushed with sudden heat as my eyes flooded with tears, spilling over. The make-believe helium in my chest rushed out, my heart deflated like a popped balloon. Would I ever meet someone who'd make me feel like Joe had?

I'd miss him so much.

Even if he said he wanted me he would be just like Austin. Eventually he'd find me lacking in some way and leave me. I'd learned the hard way that me and a man like that were ill-matched, doomed to failure and disappointment. I had to lower my expectations. Or give up.

Chapter 12

I WAS in a panic by the time I flew down the hill back to the house. I'd left Elle alone for nearly two hours while I'd met with Luis, and the sun was now quickly setting. What would she think? Though we hadn't talked about it, there was an unspoken understanding that she had to leave tonight. It was the twenty-fourth. She had holiday plans with her aunt. We'd run out of time.

What happened after that? Who knew? I had pushed the question to the back of my mind today, trying to forget that this sublime interlude with the beautiful Elle was about to end. Likely forever.

Fuck me. I didn't want to send her away. But today's developments made it even more imperative that I do so.

As if to taunt me and my willful indulgence in normalcy, Luis had delivered bad news. He'd been frustratingly cryptic during our regular video chat, saying things that didn't quite make sense about going shopping in Puerto Vallarta, the family gathering for Christmas dinner, holiday photos, and other things out of our normal context, until I cottoned on to the fact that he believed our communication network was compromised.

By whom? That was the question.

So when I heard the chopper arriving, I knew what to do. What I didn't expect was getting embroiled in a lengthy review and analysis of security footage in the storage hut, and a debate about how to handle the possible threat. Luis's team had picked up surveillance video of a group of men at a luxury hotel in PV. Between them they thought, but couldn't be sure, that the leader was none other than Juan Carlos, drug runner and my personal nemesis, who'd managed to evade detection all these years while simultaneously tormenting me.

I was the only one who'd met him in person. And if it was him, was it a coincidence that he and his thugs were poking around in my back yard? Possibly. PV wasn't such a strange place to hang out for drug dealers, despite the fact that they were based more centrally.

After studying the footage, I had to concede it might be him, but couldn't be certain either. It had been seven years, and if it was him, he'd changed. There was an eye patch that hadn't been there before, no moustache and beard so it was difficult to see his features now, and he walked with a limp. He seemed shorter. But familiar nonetheless. I just couldn't say with certainty that this was him.

But we had to be vigilant, and the team had to come up with a strategy to suss out their purpose in being here without giving anything away. Tricky.

Before the hike back down, we'd arrived at the conclusion that Elle couldn't just walk out of my compound tonight, even if she had no intention of coming back. It was too risky. So we'd come up with a further plan for Luis to come back for her later tonight and then sneak her back into Yelapa by boat in the dark.

But Elle was nowhere to be found. Not on the terrace where I'd left her, not in the main house, nor the bedroom or bathroom.

"Elle?"

Fear assaulted my bloodstream in a barrage of adrenaline, setting my nerves on fire. Where was she?

"Elle!"

Another quick dash through the house confirmed my worst suspicions. She'd given up waiting for me and left. My heart sunk in my chest, settling low in my gut like a stone, my disappointment palpable. Then, belatedly, I discovered her scratched note, barely legible, on my desk.

Goddamn it!

How the hell did she think she'd get past the electrified fence? With no clue how long ago she'd left, I ran to the concealed power box and flipped the switch, then took off down the hill as fast as I could, despite still being winded from my return. The woman would knock herself out again.

At the fence, I soon discovered how she'd done it. Clever woman. Foolish girl. And not half as clumsy as she claimed to be. Leaping over the fence, I continued down through the rough scrub and mangroves to the beach.

And there she was.

I stood hidden in the shadows of the trees, catching my breath and watching her. She was beautiful and elegant, light to my dark, the rays of the setting sun illuminating her soft, smooth curves and long slender limbs in gold. She'd gone swimming, and was just now wading thigh deep out of the water towards the shore. A glance out to the point showed that I'd barely got here in time. Another half hour and she'd not be able to pass around the rocks, yet she'd waited for me. My chest swelled with gratitude, affection, and twisted with something deeper and more painful. She'd waited, though there was nothing to wait for but a sad farewell.

She turned away to gaze out at the bay, or perhaps she was

checking the tide level at the point. Knowing I shouldn't but unable to resist, I stepped out, bending to pick up the soft beach bag she'd set on the sand, and strode towards her. Despite everything, the sight of her brought a smile to my tired face and warmed my heart.

When she noticed me, she jerked a little in surprise, then smiled as well, lighting up her face. Her relief was evident in the way she lifted her chin and dropped her shoulders. She stopped moving and reached an arm toward me.

"Join me," she called out. "The water is so refreshing. You have to feel it."

I stayed where I was, jaw tight, glancing at the sky and up and down the beach. This was precisely what we should not be doing right now with the increased threat that my enemy was looking for me.

"No one is watching. It's just us."

I wish that were true. Tense, reluctant but unable to resist her charms, I kicked off my sandals, dropped her bag, and stepped to the edge of the lapping waves. The cool water on my hot, tired feet was indeed entrancing, and a shocking sensation after so many years. But it was the curvy woman in the swimsuit, like a fifties movie star, her skin glistening wet, that compelled me to go further.

She was so beautiful and carefree, I couldn't stop myself from stepping close to her and wrapping my arms around her slender waist. She pulled me in, wrapping her arms and then her legs around me, leaning in to kiss me. Her skin was cool from the water, and slippery as satin, and with her clinging to me, I walked us out deeper and plunged under the crystal water.

She was right. It was a tragedy that I'd been living here and deprived of this sensual indulgence. It made me ponder whether an occasional midnight swim would have been so very dangerous, or if in fact I'd been punishing myself by ensuring my pleasures were minimal. As if deprivation or asceticism could make up for my guilt.

It was impossible not to smile as we swam, drifting apart and coming together again and again in the gentle rays of the setting sun. I kissed her deeply, plunging my tongue into her mouth, hungry to convey my need, and she clung to me, her hot core pressing against my belly, tempting me.

After the kissing overtook the swimming, and my need for her grew unbearable, I walked us out of the surf and lay her down on the damp firm sand at the margin of the receding tide, covering her with my body, pressing as much of my skin against hers as humanly possible. It was unimaginable that I could, that I must, let her go. Unthinkable, that I would never see her again.

And yet, it was so.

Peeling our swimsuits off and tossing them aside, I licked the salt water from her jaw, her shoulder, her collarbone and then took her glorious breasts in my hands, sucking them into hard peaks until she twisted and moaned under me.

Lifting my face to gaze into hers, I kissed her mouth, shaking my head and smiling ruefully. "I have no condom with me."

"I don't care, Joe. Take me anyway. It's all right. I have to feel you one more time."

"What if…?"

"It doesn't matter. Nothing matters now. We're both okay, and if a child should result from this one time, I'd welcome it. At least I'd have part of my dream come true."

I shook my head in feeble protest. That would not be all right. But right now, I couldn't think that through. I'd make it all right, somehow. For now, I simply had to possess her. My Elle. To show her what she'd come to mean to me, in such a short time. "I wish I could make all your dreams come true, my darling."

"And I wish I could save you from your ghosts and free you

from your prison," she whispered against my neck, dragging her tongue along my skin.

Wordlessly, she lifted her knees, opening and welcoming me, and I slipped inside her as we joined together one last time, tenderly, exquisitely, intensely. I tried to keep it slow, but my anguish at letting her go, at losing her, overcame me and the force of my feelings made me drive into her powerfully, again and again, burying myself in her as if leaving a piece of myself with her to carry away. She welcomed my demands, raising herself up to meet me, throwing her head back, opening her lips to the sunset, my name a plaintive cry on the air, giving way to keening wails as she crested.

My own climax seized me by the spine and rocked through me like thunder, the clap of my release exploded out of my throat like a war cry, blinding me.

My head spun with stars, my body spent, my face pressed to her breasts in absolute surrender, gasping for breath.

The low angle of the sun caught our attention and sharpened our awareness of the time. We rallied, standing up, brushing the sand from our skin, rescuing our suits from where we'd tossed them and covering ourselves.

Elle stood facing me, her fingers loosely laced with mine, her eyes huge and filled with sadness. "I have to go."

Longing to keep her with me, I blurted, "We came up with a plan. Luis can fly you out of here and bring you back by boat. It's safer."

She shook her head ruefully, and I knew it was ridiculously elaborate and she'd decline. She lifted one arm and let it flop down. "I've stayed too long. It's only a fifteen minute walk. No one knows me, Joe. Nobody will even notice me on the deserted path. I'll be fine."

She was right. She needed to break ties with me sooner than later. The less she knew about me and my organization, my staff, the less involved she was in my life, the better she'd be. I nodded, swallowing the lump that choked my words.

"Go now. Quickly."

She bent to strap on her sandals, and stood on her toes to press her lips softly against mine, and I answered, tasting her one last time. "Good bye, lovely wild man. I wish we'd met under different circumstances."

I nodded again, my throat tight. How I wished that were true.

I felt myself buckling, my resolve crumbling like sandstone, my mind scrambling for reasons why it was all right for her to stay. Ways to make that possible.

But she had to go, there was no room in my life for love - I couldn't bear the thought of loving and losing someone again - and my life was too dangerous for her. As long as Juan Carlos was out there, his vendetta burning strong, I couldn't put her at risk.

I stood on the sand and watched her turn and walk to the point, disappearing around it. Then I stepped back into the protection of the jungle, retreating to the cover of trees, behind the bars of the mangrove, standing still as a big cat in a cage. Unable to move away, I stood a long time as the light slowly faded to violet, watching the tide flow in, cutting off my little bay from the outside world.

As I climbed back to the house, the loss of Elle's bright presence in my life pressed down on my chest with the weight of a mountain, squeezing the breath from my lungs. How would I go on now, without her? I hadn't been able to feel such breadth and depth of emotion for years. Now, just as she'd awakened in me the power to feel, she was gone. I was alone again.

Tomorrow was Christmas. I remembered what it was like to lose my beautiful young family. Seven years ago. They died because of me. My actions. My decisions. My choices. I'd failed them. I wouldn't make the same mistake again. My attraction to

Elle was powerful, and I felt a compulsion to protect her. I couldn't tolerate the thought of someone hurting her, especially because of me. She'd be far better off without me. And she was so sweet and lovely, I knew she'd eventually find the love she was looking for elsewhere, far from my dark ugly world.

And I was familiar with the taste of loneliness. I'd grow accustomed to it again.

Chapter 13

ELLE

THE HIKE BACK to Muriel's house took longer than it should have. I didn't have my stamina back yet. After a few minutes, my head began to throb again, and picking my way along the rough narrow trail seemed much harder than it was before. The time passed in a blur, my thoughts on the beach with Joe.

Only when I turned up her garden path did I notice the tears that covered my cheeks. Pausing, I rubbed my face and caught my breath before venturing up.

A glorious rosy sunset had emerged as I'd walked back, and I stood a moment soaking in the view, reflecting on the past three days.

What would I say? What could I possibly tell Muriel about my missing days?

That I'd managed to get into trouble again?

But that this time I'd been rescued by a mysterious, danger-ous, handsome mountain man? That we'd become friends, shared our deepest secrets, and — fallen a little bit in love? Had we?

Had all that been possible in a mere three days, or was it a dream? Maybe my head injury was worse than I thought, and I was delusional.

What would I say to Muriel to explain my absence? The truth was a secret, but I had to say something.

Though the events of the past few days sounded fanciful, the emotions that swirled inside me were real. My throat closed up again, fresh tears stinging my eyes. My feelings for Joe were real. How could life be so unfair, to bring us together, to give us all that we'd shared, and then to rip it away? My sense of loss, of betrayal and abandonment was complete.

Was I really unworthy of a happy ending of my own? Were my simple dreams unreachable? What was wrong with me that fate treated me so cruelly?

"Ah, there you are, Eleanor."

I glanced up. Nobody called me Eleanor but Muriel. She was just where I'd left her, bent over her typewriter at the wobbly wood table overlooking her garden, a single candle flickering in the evening light.

"I'm almost done for the day. Just a few more notes to make and I'll be done with this part. Have you been enjoying yourself?"

Hadn't she noticed I was gone? For goodness sake? How self-absorbed could the woman be?

"It was — fine," I replied weakly, stepping into the dim interior. A gas lantern glowed from the kitchen table which was covered cheerily in a striped red woven blanket, another version of the type Joe kept on his bed, and covered me with so tenderly. I stopped in the middle of the room, my chest buckling again with a sudden silent sob. Had I dreamt it all?

"Did you have anything planned for dinner, Muriel?"

No reply came but the *ka-chunk ka-chunk* of her old typewriter keys, and I sighed heavily, heading to the bathing area to clean up and find something different to wear. I was thoroughly sick of my swimsuit, and though I had a lovely new sundress rolled neatly into my beach bag, I didn't think I had the heart to wear it. Not yet, anyway.

When I re-emerged, Muriel had covered her typewriter and tucked away her day's pages in a leather folio, setting her wide-brimmed straw hat on top of the work, ready for another day. I had no doubt she'd attempt to squeeze in a few minutes of writing even on Christmas Day.

In the kitchen, she bent and pulled out a bottle of tequila from under her counter and then reached up for two bubbly blue glasses, bringing them to the table. "I bought some bacalao stuffed tamales from a neighbour woman for dinner. There will be an abundance of food at the pot luck tomorrow, so I thought we could keep it simple today."

I turned to face her, inexplicably touched that she'd given it any thought at all. "That sounds lovely." My voice emerged faint and warbly, despite trying to act normally. "I think. What's bacalao?"

"A traditional cod mixture. Some shrimp maybe. I didn't ask Concha. She's a very good cook though. I buy from her often."

She'd done no decorating for the holiday, unless you counted the red blanket with its green and blue stripes. But for the faint refrain of Feliz Navidad drifting our way on the evening air, there was no sign of festivities in this house.

"Sit down. Join me for a toast." She sat herself, pouring out two small glasses of tequila, pushing one towards me.

I slid into the chair opposite her, smiling and taking the glass. Lifting it to my lips, I wet my mouth with the unexpectedly smooth liquor. "This is good."

Muriel nodded, taking a swig. "I buy the good stuff." She set her glass down. "So where have you been?"

"I — uh, I popped up to Puerto Vallarta. It was sponta-neous. I just wanted to do a little shopping for gifts. Also —" Suddenly I remembered the paper stars and mini piñatas. I'd actually bought folded paper stars in the marketplace of Puerto Vallarta the day before I came here on the boat. I rose and went to my room to find them. I rummaged in my suitcase, pulling them out. Muriel wouldn't know I hadn't just got them. "I thought it would liven the place up a little for the holidays," I said, returning and setting them on the table.

She lifted one, examining it, then peered closely at me. I suppose she wondered where I'd stayed, but it seemed plausible to me. More likely than what actually happened. "Would you like to hang them up?"

I nodded, glancing around her house. "It's too bad we can't have a Christmas tree. It feels strange to me."

"Hm." She screwed up her face, squinting out to the terrace. Then she went out and returned with a small leafy tree in a pot and heaved it onto the table. "I suppose this little fellow can support a star or two."

A few tiny green lemons or limes clung to its spindly branches." It's sweet." I pulled the decorations from their acetate packages and arranged them on the little tree. The branches drooped under their weight, but the effect was quite charming. "It looks like a Charlie Brown tree."

Muriel chuckled. "Indeed it does." She took another drink of tequila and leaned back, looking relaxed for the first time since I'd arrived. "How would you like to spend this evening? Any silly family traditions you're missing?"

I took a deep breath, thinking about the usual chaos at home this time of year, and let it out slowly. The house too full of people, the tables groaning with an excess of rich and sweet food, loud conversations competing with the same old sound track of Mariah Carey, Eartha Kitt and Dolly Parton's Christmas album. And the same tomorrow and the next day. Given my mood, this peaceful simplicity suited me fine.

I shook my head, smiling sadly. "When was the last time you

joined Mom and the family for the holidays, Muriel? Do you ever think of flying up?"

She guffawed. "Lord, no. That's not for me."

"Don't you get lonely?" I felt my chin quiver slightly, and lifted my glass to drink and hide it.

"Sometimes." Her gaze wandered to the ceiling and around the room. "But I'm content here. I like my life and enjoy my own company. Do you think I wouldn't change something about it if I didn't?" She faced me again, dipping her chin and peering at me, amusement crinkling her eyes.

"I suppose not." I shrugged, and felt my eyes sting.

"Besides, I have you this year to bother me."

I laughed softly at her gruffness, which felt tonight more of an affectation than any genuine annoyance, and dropped my gaze to study the woven pattern of the striped blanket, plucking at a pulled thread. "I hope I haven't been too much of a burden."

"Nonsense. I've hardly seen you. You've done a fine job of entertaining yourself."

If only she knew.

"Come on now. What would make you feel better about being here this year?"

Of all the things that I'd left behind, there was one warm, clear memory that popped into my head. "You know what I might actually miss?" Muriel's eyebrows rose in question. "Even though it's so sweet I almost have to lie down after I eat it, I don't think it would feel like Christmas without Mom's spiced apple cake with caramel glaze."

"Hah!" Muriel threw back her head in delight. "I haven't eaten that since I was —" She shrugged. "Well, I don't know. In my twenties, perhaps."

"How is that possible? Mom would've been only a teenager."

"Well, where do you suppose she learned to make that cake, my dear?"

"From you?" I asked, skeptical.

She pished. "Nonsense. It was our mother's recipe."

"Grannie Powers?"

"Mhm. And her mother's before that. It's an old family recipe, from the south."

"Huh. It's too bad I don't know it. Just one bite of that sugary treat would cure any homesickness I felt."

"What makes you think I don't know how?"

I pulled back. "I — don't picture you baking, Muriel."

"Hmph. Well, just for the pure shock of it, that's what we'll do. As soon as we've eaten our fill of tamales, we'll bake a cake. It can be our contribution to the pot luck Christmas dinner tomorrow."

And that's what we did. Muriel reheated the tamales, and we enjoyed them, along with a mango and cucumber salad and more tequila, this time blended with brown sugar and freshly squeezed lime juice. It was delicious, and with the tequila warming my belly and loosening my limbs, I could almost forget where I'd spent the past few days. Almost. Despite all that, Joe, all alone out there at his secure compound, so near and yet so unreachable, was never far from my thoughts.

After dinner, Muriel pulled out apples, eggs, spices, aromatic Mexican vanilla, oil and canned milk. She had to puzzle a minute or two, but eventually recalled the recipe. Going through the motions of blending ingredients brought back the details for her, and I beat the eggs, sugar and oil while she measured out flour, soda and cinnamon.

"I don't often fire up this oven," she said, while I peeled apples and she chopped pecans. My heart swelled in my ribcage as we worked side by side, our conversation and laughter fuelled by tequila and the warm, familiar scents of family and tradition.

We gossiped about family members young and old, and shared stories. Though Muriel was obviously in touch with Mom, she didn't have all the dirt. And she managed to shock me with a story or two about the older generation's antics back in the day. It was the perfect balm for my broken heart and left me without a single regret about my choice to hide from Christmas this year. It turned out to be the best of decisions after all.

Though I had new wounds to heal, I had new memories as well. Between the two, I spared scarcely a thought for Austin and his sudden abandonment and betrayal. I hoped he was happy skiing with his new friends in Switzerland.

The scents of baking apples, cinnamon and vanilla filled Muriel's small kitchen, and wafted out on the night air to taunt and tease the neighbours. I wished I could share this special treat with Joe, to somehow give him a taste of my Christmas. Some positive memories to chase away his melancholy ones. When I bent to pull the hot cake from the oven, Muriel bent over me.

"What happened to your head, my dear? I just noticed."

I stood up quickly, swallowing, my mind whirling. "Oh, I nearly forgot," I laughed, and it sounded as fake as it was. I turned my attention to the cake, setting it on the stovetop to cool. I lifted a hand and ran it over the scab on the back of my head, not perfectly hidden by my hair, apparently. "I … um … ran into a street sign in town. Just me being my usual clumsy self." Another fake laugh. Shoot me.

"Nonsense. Why do you say such things about yourself?"

I shrugged, setting down the tea towel. "It's true."

She grunted. "I remember you as a little girl. You loved to twirl and dance around the yard. It made us all laugh. You were such a cutie."

I fell silent, thinking. I must have been very young as the memories were faint. Mostly I recalled becoming dizzy, falling on the lawn, soiling my dress, and all the people laughing at me. Laughing and laughing. The sensation of shame coiled in my middle. That much I recalled. That was a familiar feeling.

But I pushed the disturbing feelings aside. Nothing would spoil this lovely Christmas Eve with Aunt Muriel. It was exactly what I needed to forget Joe and move on with my life.

JOE

THE EVENING DRAGGED. Suddenly I couldn't remember how I'd managed to fill the long days this past six and half years. How had I not lost my mind with boredom and restlessness? Without Elle to distract, attract and entertain me, time moved glacially, and I found myself pacing like a caged lion, inexplicably enraged with my solitary confinement.

Every time I passed my work table, Elle's childlike note taunted me, the curled, wrinkled page torn from her ruined paperback, the letters scrawled with a blunt pencil. I'd re-read it so many times I'd memorized her words.

DEAREST JOE,

I hope you're okay. I'm out of time and worried about getting back along the path this evening. I'm going to head down now. I'll wait on the beach until the rising tide decides for me when I must go. I hope to see you, to say good-bye. To thank you. I wish you a Happy Christmas, if possible. I won't forget you.

xo, Elle

I WOULD NOT FORGET her either. How could I? She'd burst into my miserable world like a ray of sunshine tunnelling through a dense canopy of jungle trees. She'd cracked the shell I'd grown to protect myself, a barrier I'd thought was so impenetrable and strong, and turned out to be as thin and fragile as that green veneer that shielded the forest floor from the powerful tropical sun.

Images of our last moments together replayed in my mind on

repeat. Swimming. Making love on the sand. Those memories would stay with me forever.

I must have been out of my mind, though. I knew better. Had more self control. How could we have had unprotected sex, after all the fuss with the box of condoms?

We'd made a healthy dent in them once we got started. Sex with Elle was a delightful revelation, her comfort and sense of adventure seemingly at odds with her prim, conservative demeanour.

But that last time, nothing between us, skin on skin, intimate, sensual, infinitely sad as we prepared to part forever, was the most intense and powerful experience I think I've ever felt. It still baffled me that she and I had achieved such a staggering sense of closeness and trust, such a depth of feeling, after knowing each other for such a short time.

I supposed there were extenuating circumstances that amplified our feelings. My prolonged loneliness, her recent loss, our isolation. Grieving hearts lived close to the surface, raw and exposed. Vulnerable.

If I were feeling philosophical, one might believe that we'd created a life in that profound moment. And what if we had?

However slim the odds, she said she'd welcome a child into her life, but how did that make me feel, stuck here, unable to be with her? I'd ensure Luis kept an eye on her. It would torture me to receive news of her back home, reading to her students, living her life without me. But if… if there were a child, how sweet would that be? To have made something new. A child that could grow up safe and strong, away from the evil that enveloped me and my life. There was something about that I liked the sound of.

I only wished I could be a part of it.

Chapter 14

I WOKE late to the scent of strong coffee brewing.

Shuffling out to the main room, I hunched at the table sipping the coffee, willing my queazy stomach to settle down. I was unaccustomed too drinking so much.

"I'd better pass on today, I think," I said, sipping my coffee.

Muriel looked no better off than me, staring dully out to sea. "Not a chance. If I have to go, you're coming with me."

"Why do you have to go?"

She lifted one thin shoulder. "It's a small community. You have to play your part."

I groaned. "What time is the party?"

"Anytime mid-afternoon. Some people will be there even earlier."

Another feeble grunt escaped. How would I manage this? I lifted my mug, drinking deeply, praying for some relief. Some strength.

"We don't have to stay late, Ellie. Just show our faces, say hello. Once the party warms up, no one will miss us if we slip out."

I sighed, massaging my throbbing temples. "Okay." Everything about today felt dull, flat, blue. I knew it wasn't just my hangover. But anyway, what could I do about that? I had to go on and live my life. This pot luck dinner party full of strangers was as good a place to start as any.

When I couldn't put it off any longer, I washed up and looked for something festive to wear. Maybe my white peasant blouse with a sarong. The brightest, prettiest thing I'd brought with me was the fuscia batik sarong I'd had with me at Joe's, but it was filthy. I pulled it from my bag to check, as if it might have miraculously shed several day's worth of sand and sweat, but not only was it dirty and wrinkled, it smelled musty and sour.

I reached into the bag again to pull out the rolled sundress, my fingers bumping against an unfamiliar hard thing at the bottom. What the heck? I pulled out a rectangular shape to discover it was gift wrapped. The same paper and ribbon that had covered the box of condoms Joe received from his friend Luis now wrapped something else of a similar size and shape. Not quite though.

Oh. My hand flew to cover my mouth. My eyes prickled. Tears sprang from my eyes.

He'd tucked a tiny note under the edge of the paper.

"TO ELLE. Merry Christmas. From your Secret Santa."

OH, *Joe. You darling, sweet man.* When had he slipped this into my bag? With trembling lips and shaking hands, I carefully opened the edges of the present. What could he possibly have given me?

Inside I found a thick paperback novel, crisp and new. It was the same one I'd been reading, that had gotten ruined. And it had just come out not long ago. I'd bought it at the airport for my trip down. He must have asked Luis to bring it. How thoughtful. And sneaky. Secret Santa, indeed.

I smiled wistfully. And I'd given him nothing for Christmas. Nothing to express my thanks for all he'd done. Taken me home, nursed me back to health, fed me and entertained me. Healed my broken heart. Loved me tenderly. And I hadn't even told him how I felt.

Something was wedged between its pages. I flipped it open to find a single condom in its wrapper and another tiny note, his handwriting so slanted, dark and neat.

"SOMETHING TO REMEMBER ME BY. ;) *I'll never forget you. xJ*"

ANOTHER MELANCHOLY TEAR slid down my cheek, and I wiped it away. If only our situations had been different. Here was a relationship far more worthy of pursuing than any I'd wasted time on in my life so far. And yet it was impossible.

But I could wear the dress, cheerful with its printed tropical fruits, to this party. If I couldn't be with Joe, for Christmas or forever, I might as well have him with me in spirit and celebrate what we'd had, however briefly.

I found Muriel, dressed in baggy silk pants and a long sleeved shirt of deepest violet, sitting morosely at her typewriter, her hands limp in her lap. Back to her usual grumpy manner, or perhaps as hung over as me, but hardly festive or social. What a pair we made.

"I'm ready." I lifted the apple spice cake with its drizzled caramel glaze, that Muriel had set out on a charming hand-painted plate.

She stood, taking a bottle of wine and a gold scarf from the table, tucking them into her bag along with the flashlight for our return after dark. She grumbled, "Let's go and get this over with so I can go back to bed." Her tired gaze slid to mine, and despite her lethargy, I saw in them a twinkle of self-deprecating amusement. A good attitude to have, under the circumstances, and I returned her hint of a smile with a shake of my head. We'd had fun together last night, drinking, reminiscing and baking. It was all I needed for Christmas this year. But we weren't done yet.

"THE PARTY IS at the home of some friends of mine. Steve and Misha. I'll introduce you."

She led the way along the path towards the village, but before we got to the edge of town, she turned up a set of stairs cut into the embankment. I followed her up several short flights of concrete steps between jungle and garden plantings, until lights, music and the murmur of conversation reached us. We emerged onto a large patio in front of an even larger house, partially covered by a big tiled roof from which hung festive decorations. Larger versions of the paper piñata stars I'd bought, and sparkling tinsel garlands. Party lights festooned from the rafters and posts.

"Oh, my. This is quite the event!" So much bigger and noisier than I'd expected.

"Oh, yes. People around here know how to throw a party."

The music, it turned out, was live. As we moved through the crowd, the band was revealed on the far side of the patio. The music was half traditional Mariachi, half modern, and I half expected to hear *Santa Baby* and *All I Want For Christmas* in between *Feliz Navidad* renditions.

The party filled the house and spilled out into the yard, and was well underway, with people standing in clusters on the dirt floor, engrossed in lively conversation, laughter bubbling up periodically. Dozens of people mingled both inside and out, some clustered in front of an enourmous table covered with dishes of food.

I set down my cake plate near the other deserts, and picked up an empty plate, filling it with an assortment of papaya, mango and avocado salads, fresh yogurt, roast turkey, tamales and enchiladas, and traditional Russian potato salad. A separate large table held platters of carved barbecued pig, the star of the show. Seeing and smelling all of this, my appetite had returned.

We drifted to a long kitchen bar tiled brightly, and someone shoved a glass of red wine into my hand. A little reluctant, but also grateful, I took a sip as Muriel introduced me briefly to Steve and Misha, and three or four people whose names I barely heard above the noise, and immediately forgot. Then Muriel disappeared to talk with a friend, and I meandered back outside, happier in my solitude than forcing small talk or explaining my existence to anyone. I had to find somewhere to set down my wine so that I could eat.

As the minutes passed, the patio became crowded with people dressed in bright tropical colours, with hats and turbans, Hawaiian shirts and tie-dyed t-shirts, flowing sarongs, crinkled white linen trousers. These expats really knew how to express themselves, and obviously all knew each other well. It was a casual but festive party atmosphere. Too bad I wasn't in a festive party mood.

Finally I found a quiet corner of the yard at the far side of the patio, standing in the shadows. I balanced my glass on top of a railing, then nibbled on the delicious assortment of dishes, enjoying their freshness and tropical flavours, watching the eccentric people in the crowd around me.

My phone buzzed in my bag, startling me. I hadn't used it in days, except to take photos of the scenery, and its battery had died at Joe's before I'd even regained consciousness. Finding that the party hosts actually had internet, which Muriel did not, I checked my messages. There was nothing urgent. Just a few holiday greetings, and a couple from Mom.

Tannis: Merry Christmas, Cuz! Missing you so much! Hugs.

Laura: It feels weird not being together for the holidays. I'm so bored.

Mom: How are you making out with Muriel, honey? Having fun in the sun?

I smiled. I decided to send a few texts to family and friends, wishing them a Merry Christmas. I replied to Mom, saying I was having a wonderful break, relaxing on the beach, visiting with Muriel, having fun. That ought to put her mind at rest, and it was half the truth.

Then, realizing I had access to the internet, I decided to take advantage of it. More than curious, I did a quick search for Joe. Or the few vague but peculiar facts I knew about him.

I knew I didn't have more than a few minutes, but was shocked by the details that came up. It wasn't hard to figure out when I'd found the right story. Of course it had made then head-lines. The details about the attack on his family seven years ago were horrible. Shocking. Gruesome. Tragic.

I'd assumed it had taken place somewhere near here on the west coast of Mexico, but in fact it was on the other side, half way between Cancun and the Cayman Islands.

His company was called Plenitud Global Corporation, and its owner and CEO was a man named Joseph Jaimes. Joe. There was no doubt in my mind. I sighed.

"Did it hurt when you fell from heaven?"

"Excuse me?" I turned to find myself being addressed by a very tall thin man in a linen jacket, bending over to address me. I leaned back to put some space between me and his overpowering alcoholic breath, taking in his leathery skin, and slightly protruding eyes. He had to be at least ten years my senior, and appeared to have lived a dissolute life so far.

"If only half of the stars in the sky shined as brightly as your eyes."

I guffawed softly at the corny pick up line. "Do those lines usually work for you?"

"I simply speak the truth."

"Right. Well, thanks, I guess."

"I'm Geoff," he said, sticking his long fingered hand out towards me. I shifted my wine glass to my left and politely shook his hand, which he promptly pinched too tightly and brought to his lips where he planted an uncomfortably long wet kiss. "Señorita. It's my pleasure."

Jerking my hand away, I quickly switched my glass back and tucked the other hand behind my back should he get any more ideas about courting me ostentatiously. "Nice to meet you, Geoff. I'm Elle. You're a local, I presume?"

"I am, Elle. I hear you're family of Muriel."

"Um. Yes, that's right. Here for the holiday." I glanced past his shoulder at the crowd.

"And are you enjoying all that we have to offer?" His brow twitched up in query.

There was something suspiciously lascivious about the way he said that. As if he were prying into my most private business. Or offering something dirty. I cleared my throat.

"Quite. Thanks." I angled my body away from him and took refuge in a sip of wine, hoping he'd move on. No such luck.

"Have you eaten? May I fill a plate for you?"

"No! I mean, thanks but yes, I have eaten. A lot. I'm good. You go ahead."

"I'd rather stay here talking with you."

"Ah." So much for my surviving this party without talking to strangers.

"And where are you from, beautiful Elle?

"Canada," I replied vaguely, glancing away again. How did I get away from him? He had me cornered and there was no one near I could signal for help. "Vancouver!" I spat, cutting off his obvious next question before it could spill from his lips.

"And how much longer are you staying in Yelapa?" Again with the hands, sliding around my elbow.

Again I moved away, rotating to face the jungle, my back to the party, so he couldn't block my escape. "Not long now. Excuse me. I have to find my aunt."

"But–"

"Have a good night." I scurried away, taking refuge in the crowd, hoping to lose him. Good grief. I shoved through the crowd to the opposite side and headed inside the house, tucking myself in a back passageway where the lights were dim. Peering around in search of Muriel, I finally spotted her on the lower patio with a couple of older people. She was smiling and looked like she was actually warming up to the fun. Good for her.

Me, not so much. I really didn't have it in me to be polite, never mind outright friendly, tonight. Making new friends took too much energy. I wondered if it was too early to escape, and if Muriel would be all right if I left without her.

I sighed heavily, feeling defeated. Always running away, always hiding from my life. Always standing on the sidelines. I was thoroughly sick of myself. Why was it so hard for me to find a place where I felt comfortable and happy? What was wrong with me?

I'd been silently a little critical of Joe, hiding away from his life. His survival strategy seemed more difficult than facing his challenges head on. But who was I to judge? Now that I knew a little more, I could better understand the seriousness of his situation and why he might choose to deal with it by disappearing. But what excuse did I have to cower and hide? What stopped me, really, from boldly pursuing my dreams? What did I really have to lose, after all, but those dreams themselves?

Life's challenges could not be avoided. Every choice you made, even the cowardly ones, had their own consequences. In the end you had to choose the price you were willing to pay. I couldn't run from my own life anymore.

It wasn't just my family, or my failed relationship. I'd realized I'd always feel this way no matter who I was with. Despite the fun with Muriel last night, I missed my family and our holiday traditions. That sense of connectedness and belonging was important to me, but if I chose to isolate myself and feel like an outsider, that would always be my truth.

I'd stumbled, for once, upon something good. Better than good. My awkwardness and clumsiness had led me directly to the sweetest man I'd ever met, and I missed his strong arms around me.

The truth was, I missed Joe and the way he made me feel. Tightness in my chest made drawing a breath difficult. My lips and cheeks pulled in a sudden grimace. Oh, no. I couldn't cry, not here.

Joe made me feel the way Austin never had. I'd felt a genuine deep connection with him. There were few people who made me feel that way. Seen. Accepted. Adored. Laura and Tannis were the only ones. Joe was worth taking a risk for -- at least I had to try. What we'd found together was precious and I needed, at the very least, to tell him how I felt, even if he sent me away again.

So what was I going to do about it? I had to go to him. Right now. I couldn't wait another day.

Having arrived at this realization, I couldn't stand still. The noise and smells of the party closed in on me, and I stepped out to the kitchen, desperate to escape. Reaching to set my wine glass down, I searched the crowd for Muriel. But in my haste, I missed the edge. Before I could catch it, my glass toppled over, crashing to the floor. Oh, shit. How did I always manage it?

I turned away, feigning nonchalance. Maybe nobody would notice. Likely it wouldn't be the only casualty tonight.

Flapping my hands, I scrambled for some way to clean it up.

But there was little to work with. I was suddenly blooming with sweat.

But I shook it off. It didn't matter. Why was I fussing? I kicked the broken glass shards under the edge of the counter so no one stepped on them. Suddenly, it was so muggy and close, my sundress clung to my moist hot skin. I plucked at the front it, trying to catch my breath. *Calm down, Elle.* I couldn't stand this crowded space another minute. I had to get out, get some air.

I had to leave. Searching again in the crowd for Muriel, I finally found her laughing with her friends at the far edge of the patio. The through of fighting through the crowd and explaining myself was overwhelming. And I didn't want to disturb her to bother her for the flashlight. Then my eye landed on just what I needed in the corner of the kitchen counter. What the hell. Glancing around again, I grabbed it.

On my way out, I thought again about the Secret Santa gift Joe tucked in my bag. I wished I had a gift for him, to recipro-cate. To show him how grateful I was for his thoughtfulness. Passing the ravaged buffet table, I saw that half of our apple spice cake remained among the ruins, crumbs scattered over the tablecloth. Frowning, I grabbed it, then added a few handfuls of cookies and other treats, tossing a napkin over the top. These people didn't need any more food. And Muriel's plate had to go home anyway.

Even with the stolen flashlight's feeble beam to guide my way, I stubbed down the stairs and realized long before reaching Muriel's house that I couldn't continue all the way in my sandals, balancing a plate. I scooted up her path, quickly swapped out the sandals for my waterproof sneakers, yanking them on.

Then I transferred the cake and cookies to a plastic bag. Though the moon was three quarters full, it would be a treach-erous enough walk in the pitch dark without further impedi-ments. Having decided to go, I was now bristling with impatience to get there. To see him before any more of this night had gone to waste.

What I'd had with Joe was too precious to throw away as if it were nothing. Whatever fears he had were worth facing. Even if he insisted on shutting me out, I had to try. At the very least, I had to tell him how I felt before it was too late and we never saw each other again.

Picking my way along the path was frustratingly slow, but I had to take care. Falling on the rocks, or in the surf, would only frustrate my aim. After what felt like forever, alone in the dark and quiet away from all the noisy celebrations, I rounded the first rock outcropping. I was getting close, and starting to think about the stupid fence again, when murmured voices drew closer in the dark. I paused, looking out at the water, where the slosh and slap of waves on the hull of a boat drew my attention.

"Feliz Navidad, Señiorita," came a Latin accented male voice in greeting out of the darkness

"Feliz Navidad," I returned. I could just make out the black silhouette of two people in a small boat, bobbing on the water.

"Are you Elle?"

That stopped me. "Pardon?"

"We are looking for Elle Garvey."

I frowned, puzzled. Who would be here looking for me? I shone the beam of my flashlight towards them, and the man's hand came up in surprise, shielding his eyes. "Who's asking?"

"Ah, ah. So sorry to startle you, *Señiorita* Garvey. Joe is so worried about you coming in the dark to meet him. He has a special surprise for you. He asked us to give you a ride."

Joe? Sent for me? My heart kicked up with sheer joy. Joe sent for me. He missed me too. He also had second thoughts and is worried for my safety. That was so like him, my heart melted. My breath came in short bursts as tears flooded my eyes, and I swept them away with the heel of my hand, embarrassed. Joe sent for me.

"Do you guys work with Luis? Is that what—?"

"*Sí, sí.* With Luis. He sent us to find you. You come in the boat. We'll take you to see Joe."

"Now?"

"You are on your way, no? This will be much quicker. We can go around the rocks."

"Right. Right. Of course."

By this time, the man had stepped out of the bobbing boat into the shallow water, holding tight to the gunnel to steady it as the hull scraped up onto the sand. He held his other hand out toward me, palm up, gentlemanly.

"Thank you." I set my hand in his rough palm and he gripped it snuggly, balancing me as I stepped toward the boat. Gripping the edge of the gunnel awkwardly with the hand that held the baked treats, I let out a squeal as I felt him grip me around the waste and hoist me up.

"*Perdóneme,*" he murmured, helping me over the edge to find my footing inside the curved hull. "*Por favor,* sit down. You don't want to fall down."

Scrambling to plant my butt firmly on a cold fibreglass bench seat in the middle of the low slung boat, I felt him push it off the sand with a grunt and leap aboard, the boat rocking and swaying with his effort and weight. After some bit of scrambling and scraping about in the dark, the engine revved to life and the boat spun. The stern dipped, nearly knocking me off the seat, as we zoomed away from the shore.

Chapter 15

JOE

THOUGH I HAD no good reason to get out of bed on Christmas morning, I awoke early. Of course I did. The more hours to wallow in self-pity and swim in memories of my former life, my family and…oh, joy, of my brief but wonderful encounter with the beautiful Elle. My heart was as heavy as the virtual vault that had kept it locked up all these years. And the woman who'd unearthed the key had walked away, leaving me feeling raw and vulnerable.

Skipping right to essentials, I poured myself two fingers of my good Avión Añejo tequila for breakfast, but before I'd more than wet my tongue, my computer trilled with the signal that Luis was checking in.

Saved from self-loathing by the bell.

"Hey Luis."

"Boss. How you doing today?"

I grunted in reply. He was always careful not to wish me a Merry Christmas, and I was never sure if I should reciprocate. The day weighed heavily on both of us, but I know he had a family, and lived a relatively normal life outside of his responsibilities to me.

"That good, huh?"

"Maybe worse than usual."

Luis's head tilted, his eyes narrowing. "Funny. You look a little better, if you ask me."

I blew a raspberry. "How is that possible?"

He lifted one corner of his wry mouth and shook his head slightly.

"You opened all the gifts?"

I scoffed. "Hell, yes."

"You're welcome."

"Fuck off." I rubbed my face with my palms, embarrassed.

"Hey! You owe me, man."

We stared at each other in silence for a long moment. My throat thickened with emotion, and I swallowed it down and sighed. "Yeah. I really do, bro. Thanks. It was a foolish indulgence, but—"

"Just what you needed, huh?"

I nodded, sighing. "So worth it." How much it meant to me, and how much more I craved, I kept to myself.

"So… I don't get the impression she's still there. Did you abandon the extraction plan?"

I nodded again, humming. "She left yesterday evening."

Luis's smile fell, his dark eyes sad. "Sorry, boss."

I twitched my shoulders, dropping my gaze. It was inevitable. "No choice about it." I fingered the wrinkled note from Elle, swallowing down the bitter taste of disappointment and loss that kept rising in my throat like bile. Finally I found my voice again.

"It had to be. The fact that Juan Carlos is still sending regular packages …we can't take chances. You know the mad fucker is capable of anything, and he clearly hasn't forgiven or forgotten me."

Luis said, "Well, that's a two way street, Joe."

We signed off, and I went back to my liquid breakfast, but somehow no longer had the heart to get roaringly drunk. I felt like an empty shell, a ghost of myself. Everywhere I looked, I saw Elle.

The ability to lose myself in my solitary oasis was ruined now. Somehow I couldn't fathom the prospect of living alone here forever. Forever? Really? Is that what I thought I was going to do, when I'd set this sanctuary up seven years ago? I'd been so far down into my funk of grief and remorse, or maybe so far up my own ass, I'd never looked up to see that I was missing out on the rest of my life.

My life.

Unbidden, images of Lainie, Megan, and Max rose in my mind. Random moments, from different times in our life. Sadly, they'd been fading. Lainie on our honeymoon in Fiji. She always, always loved the tropics. Could never get enough vacation time in the sun and water.

Megan the day she was born. How that had rocked my world. I was a father. A father! That day, I'd sworn to myself, to the memory of my dead parents, all of my ancestors, that I'd rise to the role, that I'd be worthy. The business was no big deal then. Growing, but modest, a mere hint of what I'd build over the next decade.

Then little Max, three years later. By then … I'd been pretty engrossed in work. All about providing, competing, about succeeding. I'd kind of lost it looking back now, at the way I'd thrown myself into it at the expense of everything else.

Where would we all be now, if events had unfolded differently? If I'd made different choices. Megan would be nineteen. Ahh. That killed me. She'd be a young woman, a college student, maybe some lucky guy's girlfriend. My chin quivered, my mouth suddenly awash in saliva at the thoughts. Max would be turning sixteen. I'd be teaching him to drive, my son. Watching him become a man.

My chest heaved with a silent sob. My son. My family. All lost.

But they were gone and I was still here.

Would this existence I'd carved out for myself be the life I'd want for them if I'd been the one killed and they'd survived? No. Of course not. What a waste.

When evening fell, I was deep in my annual funk, but not so drunk I would black out. Somehow this year I welcomed the thoughts. The memories. They were, after all, all that I had left of my family. I'd spent the better part of the afternoon reclining in the chaise that Elle had used. As if that could bring her back, or make me feel closer to her.

Then the computer's chime jolted me awake, and I shot to my feet.

Why was Lu calling now? He was usually home with his own family by this time. I scrambled for balance shaking my head, and went to the computer.

"What is it?"

"Boss. A situation. You clear-headed?"

I groaned, squeezing my eyes tight and opening them wide, slapping my face and drawing a deep breath. "I'm okay. Just sleepy. What's up?"

"I'm sorry to tell you this. But we think your girlfriend's got herself into trouble."

"My gir—?" Who the … "Elle? What happened?"

"Looks like she left the gringo's Christmas party and was heading your way. Alone."

My heart stuttered in my chest, crushed by a fist of fear.

"A boat picked her up. I don't know what they said to convince her, but they headed straight out of the bay. We don't know their destination. We're looking for larger boats they might be heading for but there's nothing obvious yet. Maybe Marietas."

"Fuck! I should have insisted on taking her out by chopper. When was this?"

"Satellite picked it up about a half hour ago. We just saw it. Do you want the footage? To make sure it's her?"

"Yeah. Send it." I sat, stony, waiting for the file to download, dreading the worst. A couple of minutes later, I was peering at a grainy video image of two men in a metal boat, maybe twenty-five feet in length, slide up to one of the few sandy stretched this side of the main village beach. Then I saw her golden head reflecting moonlight, and my heart lurched. And I'm sure that was the same dress. Though the details were obscured by darkness, I knew it was Elle. Something in the way she moved, in the tilt of her head, was so familiar to me now. I just knew.

I dipped my chin. "It's her." My throat suddenly felt too tight to speak. Goddam it. Why? Why was this happening? There was no struggle. She just went to the boat and allowed them to lift her in. How did they convince her to go with them? Did they force her at gunpoint? She must be terrified.

"Get the security team out. We've got to go after her."

"If we do, they'll know for sure you're here, Boss. That's the end of it."

My hands curled into fists. "How can we not?"

Luis scowled. "They're guessing. They don't know for sure she has anything to do with you."

I ground my teeth, and my jaw clicked with tension. "If they tapped into our communications, they could know more than we think."

"We didn't talk about her. It has to be speculation."

"Not if they watched her leave last night." I shot out of my chair, remembering that I'd broken my own cardinal rule. Luis didn't know it, but I'd let my guard down. Damn it! I'd been out in the water with her, on the beach for close to forty minutes. They might even have seen us together. "We can't risk it. She's in danger no matter what."

"Right. We'll get the chopper and go have a look then. But if they're gone to a yacht offshore … " He shrugged. "Well, we can ID it, maybe call in the PV police to pursue it."

"Call them anyway for back up. I don't want to take any chances with Elle's safety."

Luis nodded. "You stay put. Don't worry about her, we'll get her. I'll take care of it."

I scowled at him, my jaw working through the risks. Don't worry?

"You stay there. Promise."

I released a frustrated gust of air, my fists clenching at my sides in futility. I knew it was me they wanted, but what did it matter if Elle was hurt? Or killed? How could I sit back and do nothing? But I said what Luis needed to hear. "Yeah, yeah. Just get going. Hurry!"

"Right. I'll keep you posted."

JOE

THEN I PACED, barely able to breathe, adrenaline blasting through my body like rocket fuel, sending my heart into over-drive. *Fuck! Fuck, I'm such an idiot!* How could I put her at risk for a few moments of pleasure? This was exactly what I'd feared. Any madman who would kill innocent children would do anything. That's what I always understood in my gut. I'd looked into his eyes and I knew. He had no boundaries. There was no limit to what he'd do to get back at me. And I'd selfishly put Elle in his sights.

It would take Luis and the team maybe a half hour to catch up to them in the chopper. But if they'd gone to a larger yacht, the chopper could do little, except maybe drop a man or two down. They'd likely be outnumbered. The police would go by boat, so it would take them longer to catch up, especially out of PV. And how many men would they send? Maybe four, tops. And that's if they took the threat seriously.

A roar burst out of my lungs and I pounded a fist on my desk with a crash. I couldn't stand this. I'd go mad with worry and frustration. I had to do something. Anything.

This was my worst fear. The reason I'd hidden, stayed away from people, didn't allow anyone close. This was worse than anything I could have imagined. Juan Carlos couldn't possibly know how much Elle meant to me. I couldn't let anything happen to her. In such a short time, I'd come to feel so much for her. I thought I'd never feel again, but she'd awakened me.

Juan Carlos would laugh if he knew he had me by the balls. Now I was vulnerable. But that was the point of it, wasn't it? Juan Carlos didn't want Elle. He wanted me. And I could save Elle simply by going out there myself. Whatever happened, I'd handle it. But I couldn't save my own ass by hiding here. Not when Elle was in danger. I wouldn't lose someone I cared about by hesitating. Not this time.

Chapter 16

JOE

THE GEARS in my mind whirled.

I had a small twelve foot tin boat hidden at the bottom of the property. Never used it. I don't even know why I kept it except if felt like some kind of lame security blanket. Luis didn't even know about it. I'd acquired it by chance, years ago when a storm had broken it from its moorings and brought it to my beach. The tiny fifteen horsepower outboard I kept tucked away in a utility shed behind the house. It would't go fast, or get me very far, but maybe …

Then I was in a blur of motion. Racing around the house grabbing what I thought I'd need. A strong flashlight. A first aid kit. A few essential tools. Think! I threw on more protective clothing than I'd worn in years, along with sturdy running shoes. Then got out the little outboard motor. With only a minute's hesitation, I went to my gun locker for my rifle. Instead, when I saw it, I picked up the Sig Sauer handgun. It would be easier to carry and quicker to draw if I needed it.

I still wasn't sure if I'd kill if given an opportunity. What better reason did a man need to kill another, than revenge. For seven years I'd thought about, dreamt about what I'd do if I ever faced Juan Carlos again. Would I take my chance this time? I didn't know.

Tucking it in my pocket, I prayed I didn't.

The engine was heavy, but I hauled it down to the beach. Then I went to unearth the boat, hoping it hadn't corroded. Tossing away the dry palm fronds that concealed it, pulling back the tarp, it looked to be much the same as when I'd hidden it.

Clearing the debris and tarp away, I hoisted the small boat onto my shoulders. Fuck, it was heavier than I remembered. Stumbling, I drew upon my resources, thinking of Elle, and carried it down to the beach clamping on the outboard. Then I hauled on the cord. It sputtered and died, though I knew I kept it full of fuel to keep the condensation out.

Come on! Trying again with a little choke did the trick and it rumbled to life. Thank God. Then I turned on the flashlight and pushed away from the shore. As I roared away from the beach in the little boat, bobbing over the waves, I was almost having an out of body experience. The sensations, my surroundings, were so alien.

In the ten minutes it took me to reach the edge of the village, I'd devised a plan. Dropping the revs, I bobbed quietly among the boats anchored just off shore. Everyone was at home with family or at a party tonight. I didn't worry I'd be seen by anyone. I only needed to make the right choice. Weaving in and out, I finally found what I wanted. A newer model Yamaha 210 FSH that I knew from reading had twin motors that would give me about a hundred and thirty horse output and an electric starter I figured I could hot wire. I'd compensate whoever owned it later.

Climbing aboard with my gear, I went straight for the panel and pulled out my screwdriver. Time was short and I had to catch up. There'd be little point in this if I were the last to arrive.

When I had the starter wires out, I studied them, hoping nobody had done a runaround and fucked up the wiring. That's why I wanted a newer boat. Testing for a spark against ground, I twisted the red and green wires together with my pliers and then, holding my breath, touched the blue. And the engine roared to life. Thank God.

Leaping to the bow, I cranked up the anchor and returned to the cockpit, popping it into gear and tearing out of the bay as fast as my raging heart, straight through the centre of the bay, aiming for Islas Marietas. For Elle. And for Juan Carlos. To meet my fate and whatever it held in store.

As the minutes passed, I couldn't stop the visceral memories of the attack from flooding my mind, swamping my body with adrenaline. Being on a boat, in the open sea, brought it all back. A tight twinge in my side had me remembering getting shot, and I pressed my free hand against my scar. Despite the cool breeze, I was sweating. That I was racing toward my own demise seemed inevitable. Yet I'd rather fight and die trying to save Elle than sit back and do nothing.

Hopefully I'd see lights, hear sounds, or some hint of where the action was. I couldn't see where I was heading because it was black as fuck out here.

ELLE

NOT MANY MINUTES passed before I recognized the magnitude of my mistake. *Oh, Elle. This really takes the cake.*

I looked down at the bag of apple spice cake and cookies, my hand holding the neck of the plastic bag in a white-knuckled grip along with the cold fibreglass edge of the hard seat where I hunched with my heart in my throat, my breath coming in shallow puffs.

What the hell had I just done?

I was thirty-four years old, for God's sake. Was I really this naive? This stupid? This slow?

I couldn't lift my gaze to look at the man across from me, and dare not turn to look at the guy driving the outboard motor behind me. No one spoke. My mind whirled like a dervish at the terrifying implications of my new situation.

Where the hell were they taking me in the middle of the night? Would I even see another day? The tension in my body reached maximum, and tremors shook me from the inside out. The night air was cold on my skin, and goosebumps rose up on my arms and legs. What was happening to me?

Obviously these people were not sent by Joe, nor by Luis. First of all, nobody knew I was coming since I'd only just decided. There'd been no plan for me to return, tonight or ever. *Stupid, stupid Elle!*

Secondly, he'd addressed me by my surname Garvey, which Joe did not know. We hadn't exchanged any personal information like that. It was, I supposed, possible for his omniscient chief of security to have figured it out. But I'd be fooling myself if I indulged in that kind of thinking.

Instead, I desperately needed to figure out how to get away from these guys. There was no doubt in my mind who they worked for, and what they were after. The solution, it came to me, was to convince them they'd made a mistake. That Joe and I were not friends. That under no circumstances would my capture lure Joe out of hiding.

I hung my head, swamped in shame. God, I hoped that were true.

Somehow that far outweighed any fear I had for my own safety. Though that was just as naive. Whether or not tricking me to get in their boat worked, I'd just been kidnapped late on

Christmas night in a remote village by people who I knew, I knew for a fact, were ruthless killers and drug smugglers. Why was I not screaming in terror and fighting them?

I guess this was the freeze response. Flight was not possible, at least not yet. I didn't even know where they were taking me. We roared over the waves in barely enough light to see by, the beautiful moonlight I'd admired earlier sparkling on the waves like twinkling Christmas lights, ignorant of my dire straights.

Fighting didn't seem to be an option either. I hadn't yet given them a reason to pull out guns, but I had no doubt they carried them. I swallowed thickly, my mouth suddenly as dry as dust. I licked my lips.

All I wanted was to bury my head in my hands and cry. But I didn't. I had to think, and think fast. My pulse pounded so hard I could swear it was as loud as a base drum. My ribs fairly bounced with its wild beating. *Come on, Elle. Think. Be brave.*

"W-wait until I get my hands on that asshole," I said, my voice sounding shrill and false over the roar of the outboard motor.

"What?" The guy in the bow of the boat shifted his weight, focusing his attention back on me. "Who you talking about?"

I dropped my tone to a deeper register, pushing past the stranglehold on my throat. "Joe, of course. I really appreciate the lift, guys. I'm so furious with him I could spit. Wait until I give him a piece of my mind."

He stared at me, not speaking, and I hoped I was convincing enough to give him pause. Please, please, believe me.

Instead, he said something in Spanish to the driver, who replied. They continued exchanging short comments, ignoring me. Not good.

"You're not interested in his romantic surprise?"

"Not a chance. Like he'd plan this anyway. If I see him again I'm going to... uh ... kick him in the nuts. After what he did to me? I couldn't get away from him fast enough. He's u-unstable. And thoroughly unlikeable."

His expression was hard to make out in the darkness, and I waited for his reaction, holding my breath. He said something to his companion in Spanish. Then they both burst into laughter. God help me, they laughed.

"What? You don't believe me?" I kept on, because I didn't have another plan. "You'll see. I don't know where you're taking me, but you're mistaken if you think he'll show up. He doesn't think much of me either. We had a big fight."

The guy chuckled again. "That's what you call what you were doing? Wrestling on the beach?" He translated his witticism for his companion, and they both guffawed again at my expense. I also realized, if they'd somehow seen me with Joe on the beach, my arguments were hopeless.

I'd have to bide my time until I got out of this boat, since at this point it was ride or die. At this point, it was hard to imagine my choice wasn't between drown or die. All I could do was hang on and hope some opportunity to escape presented itself. No matter what kind of risk or threat I faced, I'd do it for Joe. When it did, I'd be ready.

Chapter 17

I KNEW Islas Marietas were about twenty-two miles off shore. A little closer from Yelapa than from Puerto Vallarta. It was hard to say who'd get there first. Either was possible. Nevertheless, I rode hard, the throttle fully open, the Yamaha skimming through the crests of the waves with a hard grinding noise like a torpedo.

No other boats were visible on the half hour ride out to the islands. If they'd transferred to a yacht, it wasn't here. Or it was long gone. But my gut told me that wasn't their strategy. Not if they wanted me to find them.

So, it had to be the islands. But where would they land? There wasn't much to choose from on the flat barren rocks of Marietas. On my approach, no lights were immediately evident, but then both Playa Del Amor and Playa la Nopalera were on the far north side of both islands, opposite to my angle of approach. Which of the two small islands though?

The tide was partially in and rising. Although private and hidden from view, Playa Del Amor would be less accessible at high tide, with few options once the hidden interior beach filled with sea water. Whereas, Playa Nopalera was more open, and there was a ladder leading up to the barren plateau above the rocky bluffs. If it were me, I'd choose the latter. If I were correct, it would be easier to land the chopper there as well. I prayed I was.

Having come to this conclusion, I cut to the left as soon as the islands came into view. The rocky white bluffs emerged out of the gloom, rising up like ghostly walls in the pitch dark.

No sense wasting time circling around the further island. That's the way the Puerto Vallarta police would come anyway. This route still held the possibility of surprise. Fortunately, the moon shone brightly, reflecting off of sandstone and beach sand, giving me enough markers to guide my way. As long as I didn't ground the boat on the many rocks hidden under the surface.

As soon as I advanced between the two islands, a small flicker of light ahead caught my eye. I'd made the right call. I hoped Luis could see them from the air. There was no sign yet of the chopper or a police boat. I prayed they were not far behind me. I was ill-equipped to handle this alone, certain to be outnumbered. The hard shape of the Sig Sauer pressed into my back.

I dropped the throttle to a low hum as I approached. No sense alerting them to my presence earlier than necessary. Hopefully, they were preoccupied and I could sneak in a little closer. Wary of the rocks, I drifted in as close to the shore as I dared, hugged the coast, hoping the irregular coastline concealed me for as long as possible. I knew there were two beaches, separated by a rocky land bridge. If I were lucky, I could land in the closer one, and approach by foot through the rock arch.

Clearing the rocks, I killed the engine and slid the anchor overboard as quietly as possible. I didn't know if I'd need a getaway vehicle, or if I'd ever be leaving this barren rocky island, but it paid to keep my options open. Then I grabbed the flashlight and slipped into thigh deep water, making my way to shore.

I tried to keep my mind clear of thoughts of Elle for now. I had no idea what I'd discover, so I pushed onto the beach and edged toward the rock archway. There was water under it, but just a foot or so of surf, so I waded through, keeping to the shadows under the rock bluff, until I could peer around the edge onto the larger beach beyond.

And there they were.

A group of men, it looked like six or seven of them, huddled together. Only one held a small lantern. The dark silhouette of another man paced around the edge of the group, a separate sentry. Two long low boats rested on the beach near the water's edge. Murmured voices carried to me but I could make out no words.

Waiting and watching, I knew I'd recognize the right moment when it came. Suddenly a high feminine voice traveled across the night air piercing my heart.

Elle. My heart kicked me in the ribs, as if until this moment I didn't believe she was actually here. Low voices rose and fell. What were they saying to her? What would they do next?

One man stood apart. Smaller, he leaned on a walking stick of some kind, and despite the altered stature, I immediately knew him. Juan Carlos.

Elle pointed and stepped closer to him. "I know who you are. You're scum. You're an animal. A brute. I know what you did. And you won't get away with it."

"Shut the fuck up, *puta*!" Juan Carlos's hand came up like lightning and slapped her so hard she stumbled, falling to her knees on the sand.

Her cry of shock and pain cut through me like a machete, and I lurched, barely holding myself back from charging forward. I clenched my jaw and fists, holding on by a mere breath. But damn, that didn't stop her. She carried on berating him, though her voice carried tears, on the edge of panic.

"You're going to fail. You're finished. Joe won't come. He's not a fool, and he's not interested in me, anyway. Why do you think he sent me away? You're so stupid."

"Get her outta my face. If she doesn't shut up, make her!" Juan Carlos turned his back to Elle and strode down the beach with his limping gate, away from her, followed by a couple of his men, leaning in as if in discussion.

Elle lunged after him, but the man closest to her grabbed her arms and dragged her back. He jerked her so roughly, my gut twisted. But I had to pick a moment when they were distracted. Then I'd run for Elle.

Suddenly the dull throb of the chopper's blades bent the night air with a *whump whump*. Luis. Thank God he was close. Finally. Soon all would be chaos. I had to get to Elle before they did something desperate.

That they'd become aware of it was evident in the shifting of their bodies, the excited murmur of their voices. The man holding Elle yanked her back away from the water, toward the rock wall that enclosed the beach and I heard her voice rise along with his, in argument.

The others clambered and turned to look up and out to sea, talking excitedly among themselves.

My muscles tensed and flexed, primed for battle, and my heart pounded in my ribcage like a drum. I drew air to fill my lungs, held it and let it out slowly, trying to calm myself for what came next. My focus was absolute.

The sound of the chopper drew nearer, the volume rising.

A sudden frenzy of activity erupted on the beach. With a terrifying roar, the chopper flew over the beach, swooping and then disappearing up over the lip of the cliff above our heads. One guy fired a random shot up at it, the idiot, as if that would do anything. Then there was shouting and mayhem.

I made a run for Elle while she was isolated from the larger group, pushing hard, my wet sneakers sinking into the soft sand as I crossed the clearing. My pulse hammered loud in my ears, echoing the rhythm of the helicopter. Shouts rose up, and dark bodies shot towards me, closing in. I needed to get Elle away from them. That's all I could think about.

Within seconds, I'd drawn near the back wall, but by then several men had surrounded me, cutting me off. One lunged at me, and we tussled before I threw him off, elbowing him in some soft body part, eliciting a grunt. No sooner was I on the move again when another attached himself to me like a mollusc, clinging, his feet dragging as I bulldozed forward. I was reminded of my college football days as a linebacker. The second man was harder to shake, and I had to pause, twist, grab his arm and throw a punch in the general vicinity of his head. My fist connected with a painful crack, sharp pain shooting through the bones of my hand. He fell back, and I turned again, searching for Elle in the gloom.

Smart girl, she took advantage of the moment to kick the guy grabbing her. In the frenzy, she slipped her keeper and ran to the ladder.

Another sentry turned back and saw her too, raising his arm, pointing, the silhouette of a gun in his hand.

In desperation, I shouted, "Hey! Stop!" as loudly as I could to distract him. He spun and lunged in my direction just as two more closed in on me from the side.

He hollered for help. Another guy went to follow Elle up the ladder but Juan Carlos's voice cut through the noise. "Let her go. Stay down here. There's a boat approaching."

Relieved, I saw her bright, lithe form clambering up, the moonlight reflecting off of her dress and light hair. I prayed the chopper was able to find a landing spot up there on the grassy plain, and Elle would make it. I hoped she didn't stumble into a bed of prickly cactus in the dark.

Abruptly, I was overpowered, three men holding on to me, holding me back, a fourth hovering close by. Lifting my gaze, I made out the outline of Elle topping the ladder against the sky, disappearing over the lip. For now, no one chased her. Instead, they all focused on me, their ultimate prize. I hoped Elle would be all right, and Luis would find her. At least I'd accomplished that much.

ELLE

FRANTIC, I pushed off the last rung of the ladder and crawled onto the dusty ledge at the top of the bluff, my heart racing. Only then did I dare look back over my shoulder to see if he was in pursuit. But, amazingly, no one had followed me up the ladder. I scrambled back and to the side a couple of yards and dropped to my stomach, flat, peeking over the edge at the sudden chaos that had erupted on the beach below me.

My panic at being dragged from the boat onto this dark secluded beach, and realizing there were at least another four or five men here, drove me near hysteria. The cool calm I'd feigned on the boat ride completely disintegrated, and found myself screeching at them, fighting every hand that grabbed me, resisting their efforts to push me around. I knew I didn't have any hope, and instinctively decided to be the biggest pain in the ass hostage I could be. I might have made the ultimate mistake of my life, but I wouldn't go down without a fight.

Especially when I saw the slimy little pirate who seemed to be their leader. Was this pathetic man the demon that had killed Joe's family? My blood ran cold then hot with rage that I couldn't contain. Something told me an angry hysterical woman would confuse them a little, and it might buy me time to figure something out. Or, dare I hoped, that someone would come to my rescue? I had no reason to assume so.

But then, while we were squabbling and scrapping, the

sound of the helicopter broke up the party, sending every man there into a frenzy of panic. A chopper! It had to be Luis. Didn't it? Why else, who else, would be here, now, in the middle of the night on Christmas? Please, please let it be the all-seeing, all-knowing Luis.

I took my chance when I saw it, flailing and kicking at my captor, luckily breaking away just when his attention was snagged elsewhere. Then, I just ran for it. I had no idea what I'd find at the top of this ladder, but it seemed my only option.

What I found was a flat, grassy plateau, now floodlit with the swaying twin spotlights of the helicopter, hovering in search of a level spot to land, blindingly bright if I looked at them. Two men rappelled down ropes the short distance, leaping to the ground.

Now, looking down at the utter mayhem below, I saw that they'd completely lost interest in me, totally consumed by new problems. The sound of the helicopter was loud behind me, the gust of wind from its blades whipping at my hair and skirt, sending clouds of dust and sand into the air. I tucked my face down onto my arms, my mouth and eyes closed tight, rubbing them clear.

In the centre of the scene below, the criminals closed in on one man, larger than most. After a scuffle, three or four of them held him down, and the creepy pirate with the eye patch stepped up close to him, sneering.

They exchanged words too low for me to hear over the helicopter's roar. But something in the tone of voice, the way he carried his body, the way he lifted his bearded face to the sky, peering in my direction, told me the man on his knees was Joe. An involuntary scream forced its way into my throat. "Joe!"

He came after me. It was both wonderful and terrible. How could he come here when he must have known that it was a trap set for him? I didn't know what to feel, except overwhelm and fear, and something deep and tender underlaying it all. That he would risk it all for me.

I wanted to be with him, though I knew I couldn't help. I crawled closer to the ladder, fearful but determined. There was no point in going back down, except to show him that I cared. I could do that much.

Just then another boat zoomed toward the beach, its glaring headlight cutting a path through the darkness. A commotion rose behind me. Hushed voices and thumping foot falls neared me as more men leapt ashore below, shouting, and the main group dispersed. A hand came down on my shoulder, stopping my movements cold, my heart leaping to my throat. I screamed.

Peering up revealed a calm, dark-haired, square-jawed man. "Stay here please, Elle."

I withdrew and cowered, retreating into the darkness as he and two other men rushed towards the cliff edge and the ladder, two of them disappearing down it, the third lying on his stomach at the edge of the cliff with a rifle pointed over. He seemed unaware that I lay but a few yards from him in the dark. I could hardly breathe I was so terrified.

Then they were all running in different directions, either to escape or in pursuit. In the darkness, I could barely tell who was whom. Especially when gunshots were fired. At that point, I was screaming and flinching with every loud noise and sudden violent movement, though no one could hear me above the racket.

I kept my eyes locked on Joe, or tried to. I lost track of him, searched, then found him again in the scramble of bodies. That's when I saw him pull out a gun and point it at the pirate.

JOE

• • •

FINDING MYSELF SURROUNDED, my arms held tightly, despite my best efforts to shake them off, I stumbled and dropped to one knee. Then the cold butt of a pistol pressed against my neck, and I stopped moving, my heart galloping like a herd of wild horses in my chest. I turned my head away from the gun, seeking my enemy among his thugs.

And there he stood.

He laughed. "I knew you'd come. You're so predictable Captain America."

I yanked again at my captors grips in frustration, and there was another scuffle as they shifted and tightened their grip. The pistol pushed harder against my neck, accompanied by a low growling voice near my ear. *"No muevas, pendejo."*

Juan Carlos limped closer, planting his walking stick in the sand, tilting his head to study me. Gritting my teeth, I lifted my gaze to glare back at him, my gut swirling with hatred.

He grabbed the lantern from his man and held it high, illuminating both our faces, and those of the men around him in a weak halo.

"You look a little less polished than the last time we met, Jaimes." He grinned, enjoying his moment of power. "Life been a bit hard for you, has it?"

He'd changed, too. The eye patch from the security footage was there, the facial hair, the walking stick to aid his limp, and now that I saw him up close, a missing third finger on his left hand. He also didn't have the bling he used to wear, or the expensive threads, as if he weren't exactly flush with money. "Looks like you're the one who's been worked over. Your clients weren't too happy with you, I guess?"

He sneered at me, flicking his fingers, and I guessed I'd hit a tender nerve. Also new, the mad glint in his one dark eye that struck me as not so much intelligent as crazed. Obsessed.

I panted, winded and overcome with a sudden fury for this

evil creature who'd taken the lives of my innocent family. "I'm glad. I hope you bled, you worm."

He curled his lips and nodded. "I'm not so easy to stop. And I never forget those who did me wrong. Finally, we…" He gestured back and forth between us, as if there could be any confusion about who was facing off here, "… finish this business between us. I've waited too long to regain my proper place."

I could hardly find words to express my feelings towards him. "You took more than your revenge seven years ago, Fucker. It's you that owes me."

He laughed again. "Too bad it's not going to turn out that way, hey, gringo?" His men chuckled and I prayed Luis and my guys had landed and would show up soon. Otherwise, I was screwed.

Stalling for time seemed a good strategy, under the circumstances.

"You seem to take delight in hurting innocents, Juan Carlos. I think it's time you paid for your crimes."

"We'll see about that, Jaimes." He turned and murmured instructions to the man on his right, and suddenly I saw stars as something hard slammed against the side of my head. I collapsed to the side, pulling a couple of my captors with me into a tackle. Freeing a hand, I lifted it to the side of my head, feeling for blood as my vision swam with stars. Fuck, that hurt like a sonofabitch!

Just then, shouts rose up behind the group. Most of them turned and ran off, and I presumed that Luis and his men had dropped down the ladder from above. A sharp gunshot rang out in the night.

Men ran in every direction, and I took the chance to rip away from them, pulling the pistol from the back of my pants, trying to focus my eyes after that blow to the head, hoping the old Sig Sauer still worked and wouldn't blow my hand off.

Another shot rang out, and then the ping of metal rang through the air as the bullet bounced off the ladder. More shouting from different directions, and I realized then that the PV police boat had arrived on shore, and more men ran onto the beach.

Juan Carlos lurched off for one of their boats with a couple of guy.

Before he could disappear from my sight, I raised my own pistol in his direction. I couldn't let him escape, leaving his men to finish this fight while he slunk off into the night. He wouldn't get away this time.

But I was no killer. Despite the opportunity, and the fact that no one would blame me, I wouldn't to it. I felt nothing but contempt for him, and still had enough pride in myself to not lower myself to his level. Instead, aiming steadily for his thigh, I pulled the trigger, the force slamming back into my arm, watching him jerk like a puppet as the bullet hit. That ought to slow him down.

His men turned on me, shouting.

A hot hammer slammed into my chest like a battering ram. What the hell? Was that the recoil? I turned to look around for what had slammed into me. Another sharp shove into my shoulder had me suddenly on the ground, face first. Stinging fire exploded in my chest, knocking the air from my lungs with a loud grunt. I gasped for breath, scrambling to get up, but I couldn't find my footing and kept falling over, suddenly ungainly as I staggered forward and fell again.

"Joe!" Was that Luis? "Joe!"

"Luis!"

I flailed, trying to get up. Where was he? Bright lights flashed back and forth across the beach, blinding me. I staggered, tripped, fell down again.

After that, things got really quiet. I was the still centre of a storm that raged around me. The details blurred, the noises blending into unintelligible muffled sounds as my mind narrowed, focussed on gasping breaths, grunting with each effort. Confused, I listened hard to make sense of the sounds and movements around me.

Then suddenly I was being hoisted into a harness. Blinking in bright lights, I peered up into Luis's familiar face.

"We've got you, Boss. It's gonna be all right. Hold on now."

Something held me down. My chest was tight with pressure, and breath still wouldn't come. "Where's Elle?" I gasped. Where was my voice? Where was she? "Did you see her? Don't leave her. I've got to see Elle."

My last thought was that I'd failed again. I'd failed to save her and I was dying. This is how it should be. I should be the one to die to save the one I loved.

"Don't worry, Joe," were the last words I heard before everything faded to darkness.

Chapter 18

ELLE

I WAS KEENING LIKE A CHILD, crying, gasping, knowing I was hysterical but unable to stop as the men hoisted a limp Joe up off the ladder in a canvas harness. He'd been shot. I'd seen it happen. Unbelieving, I saw him jerk, stumble, jerk again and fall.

My ears were deaf to the constant shouts and gunshots, my head ringing with echoes, my own pounding pulse the loudest sound. I saw Juan Carlos go down, as did a couple of others, and then everything happened so fast. Joe fell. My heart stopped as he lay on the sand unmoving while the police and Luis and his men rounded up the thugs.

Help him. Someone do something. Please.

Then it was over.

The police rounded up the criminals, loading them into boats, pushing off into the night, their headlights fading into the distance. Suddenly the beach fell into darkness and silence. Had I imagined the entire episode?

Up on the plateau, Luis's men carried Joe to the helicopter. He was unconscious. Was he even alive? I couldn't breathe.

I kneeled on the ground, watching everyone rushing around me. Frozen to the spot, I was numb as the event replayed in my mind over and over. Joe. Joe jerking with the impact of bullets. Joe falling.

"Elle."

I looked up, startled. It was the square-jawed guy again.

He set a gentle hand on my shoulder. "We should get going."

Still I stared at him dumbly.

"I'm sorry. I'm Luis. I thought you knew."

I nodded. A tiny noise came out of me, but no voice. No words.

"You're in shock. Come on. Let's get our man to the hospital."

Suddenly I sucked in a gasping breath. Then another. I let him lead me across the grassy plain toward the helicopter. He set a warm hand on top of my head and I bent over, going where he led me, through the open side doors.

Then I found myself for the first time in my life inside a chopper, disoriented. I don't know what I expected, but there were bucket seats, just like on a plane. Most of them were full, and I got my first look at the other members of the security team.

Joe was laid out on a bare section of the cabin behind the rear pair of seats, which looked like a cargo area, with straps on the walls. One of the men squatted beside him, bent over him.

I was gently pushed down onto a seat.

"Sit tight," Luis said, fastening a seat belt around me, then he joined them in the back as the other guy ripped open Joe's shirt, applied wads of gauze and pressure to his bleeding wounds as the chopper lifted off.

Then we rose into the air and swooped, turning in a wide arc and heading into the night.

I kept my eyes glued to Joe. He was alive. He twitched a little, and then moaned, barely conscious, but I was never so happy to see signs of life, however feeble. My breath came in short shallow bursts, and tears stung my eyes as I looked on.

"Do they know what they're doing?" I asked nobody in particular.

The man beside me grunted. "We've all got basic first aid tickets."

That was good, I guessed, but this seemed to be far beyond the skill level of anyone here. I caught only glimpses, but there was blood everywhere, soaked through Joe's shirt, on the gauze, on the hands of the man beside him.

Joe moaned again, turning his head back and forth. He was barely conscious.

"Get Elle. Don't let anything happen to her."

"We got her, Boss. Don't worry."

"Elle!" He jerked, trying to sit up, but his caregiver pushed him back down.

"Stay still, Boss," he said.

"Where's Elle? I want to see her."

Luis glanced my way, gesturing to come back. I unclipped my belt and got up, hunched over, and wedged my way through the gap between the seats. There was barely room for me, but I knelt on the floor as close to Joe's prone form as I could get.

"Joe," I said, my voice a thin cry. "I'm here." The metallic scent of blood filled my nose, and my tears flowed, blinding me.

His hand shot out, grabbing for me, and I took hold of it. He was sticky with blood, and gritty with sand, and the best thing I'd touched all day. I hugged his hand to my heart, squeezing him. "Elle," he croaked. He was delirious, incoherent, mumbling some words I couldn't make out.

"Take it easy, Joe. Lie quiet. We'll be at the hospital in no time, buddy," Luis whispered. I believed him, but I also heard the fear in his voice, and it amplified my own terror.

"I'm here Joe." I threw myself forward, getting my face as close to Joe as possible, hoping he could see me. His eyes were glassy, and I could hear his shallow, rasping breath. "Joe, Joe. I'm so sorry. It's all my fault. I'm so stupid. I'm so sorry, Joe. I'm sorry I crashed into your life and ruined everything."

He stared at me for a long minute, his blue eyes shadowed and unfocussed, then his eyes slid closed, his head lolling weakly. "I'm not, angel." Then he went completely limp, his breath gurgling.

"Nooo!" A keening cry tore out of me and I pulled his hand to my lips. "Joe, can you hear me? Joe! Please don't die, Joe. I love you."

My heart shattered into a million pieces, pain shooting through my body.

I came back to tell him how I felt about him. But seeing him now, he meant so much more to me than I'd realized. What were the chances that two lonely souls destined to meet would find each other in the remote tropical jungle? If only I could go back, could have another chance, I realized that love was worth taking risks for. It was so rare and special and made living worthwhile. Risk was nothing if you had a worthy reason. Now it was too late. I'd lost my chance again.

Now that I'd found him, how would I live without him?

"I don't know what the hell happened in just three days," Luis grumbled, shaking his head.

Chapter 19

JOE

UGH. Everything hurt. Especially my head. I groaned.

"Hey, Boss. Welcome back."

I cracked my eyes open. "Mmm." My eyes darted around, trying to make sense of my surroundings.

"Puerto Vallarta hospital. You've been out since your surgery."

I grunted again, piecing together what facts I could remember. I tried to lift an arm to touch my chest, remembering the fire, but I couldn't move it. I was hogtied with bandages.

"Don't try to move. You caught two bullets. One through the chest, just missed your lung, and the other in the left shoulder. That's the one that probably hurts."

I let my head drop back onto the pillow. I was alive.

I was afraid to ask "Juan Carlos?" I looked toward Luis, standing at my side.

"Dead."

I frowned. "I shot his leg. I think."

Luis grunted affirmative. "The police took him down. And a couple more. The rest are locked up."

I released a sigh of relief, trying to swallow, my mouth parched as dust.

Luis lift a cup of water to my lips and I sucked the straw, licking my dry lips, tasting bitter chemicals. My throat hurt, and my voice was reluctant. I whispered, "Ours?"

"Everyone's good. Just scrapes and bruises. They did great."

I swallowed tenderly. "Unbelievable."

"Yeah. It's finally done."

I rocked my head from side to side. "Should have lured that fucker out years ago."

Luis guffawed. "I guess you had to wait for bate."

I stiffened, frowning, feeling tightness on my face. "Elle. She okay? Where'd she go? Is she gone home?"

Luis scoffed, laughing quietly, shoving his hands into his pockets, rocking back. "I still don't know what the hell happened between you two, but she's just as bonkers about you as you are about her."

I gritted my teeth, sliding my gaze to his face again. "What?"

Luis jerked his head towards the door. "She wouldn't leave. She stayed right here all night."

My heart lurched in my chest, a burst of happiness flooding through me. "She's here?"

"Mm. We sent someone to tell her aunt, brought her here too. They're just gone for a coffee."

I drew a ragged breath, feeling sudden emotions swamp me. My eyes stung, and I felt my lips tremble.

Luis's hand came down on my good arm, squeezing. "I'll give you a minute. Why don't I go tell her you're awake."

I nodded, swallowing down salty tears, closing my eyes.

Alone, I asked myself what I was feeling? What I was doing? What would happen now?

Everything had changed, would change. I didn't even know who I was anymore. There was so much to sort out.

Some minutes passed while my thoughts spiraled.

Then the door opened, and she stepped through. Our eyes met, and time stopped as a world of thoughts and feelings flew between us. Then she was beside me, touching me, and I swore I levitated, all my pain disappearing in an instant.

"Hey, you."

She burst into tears, her trembling hands cupping my face, stroking gently. She shook her head, then bent it, bringing her face to my bandaged chest, her hair falling forward in a curtain. "I'm so sorry."

"What are you sorry for, angel? Bringing me back from the dead?"

She lifted her head, her face inches from mine, her big brown eyes wet with tears. "I nearly got you killed, you idiot. What are you saying?"

I filled my lungs and sighed. "I'm saying … that I'd rather be here with you now than back at my estate all alone. I'm saying … that I was as good as dead before you found me."

Her lips quivered, and she licked the tears from them before pressing her mouth softly against mine.

"There. You see. I'm all better now."

"I'd smack you if you weren't already such a mess."

"You better not."

She sobered. "Seriously. I told you I was trouble. This is the worst thing I've ever done. I'm so sorry I got in that boat, you'll never know."

"Did you hear, he's dead?"

She nodded.

"That's a gift. I have my life back, now."

She stood up, taking my hand between hers, lacing her fingers in mine. "What will you do with it?"

It was overwhelming, all I had to deal with. I didn't know

where to begin. I drew in a breath. "Too much to think about right now."

She nodded.

"Muriel came here?"

She made a funny face. "She did. We kind of bonded when I got back. But then, I couldn't stay away."

"I'm glad. When do you fly back to Vancouver?"

"Tomorrow." Her voice wavered, as if the thought of parting brought her as much sorrow as it did me.

"Some vacation, huh?"

"Well." She looked out the window, smiling wryly, then back at me. "I haven't given Austin much thought, that's for sure."

"Good. I don't want you to waste another minute thinking about that loser."

"What should I think about?"

"Think about … when we can see each other again."

Her eyes met mine, confused, questioning, uncertain. She didn't speak.

"Don't you think … " She shrugged, and I saw her insecurities return, and her doubts manifest on her face in worry, in her slouched posture.

"I think, as soon as I'm able, I'll be visiting you in Vancouver. That's what I think. So you'd better be leaving your phone number with Luis or I'm going to be awfully disappointed."

She was crying again, the tears tracking down her cheeks. When she tried to speak, she failed, her voice shaking and giving out. I was content just to look at her, my heart swelling in my chest as if it might float up and away.

There'd be time, to tell her all the things I felt now. I thought I was keeping others safe from danger but I was cowering, I was hiding, letting life pass me by, unwilling to risk my heart again. That's the truth. Now, I had so much living to do. So much lost time to make up for.

I tugged on her hand until she took the hint and leaned over me again. I lifted my chin, and she lowered her mouth to mine. It wasn't much of a kiss, but I'd make up for that later, too.

"I think I'm a goner."

She sniffed. "What?"

"I've fallen for you, lady. Big time."

Again her mouth quivered. "Thank you for the book. You're the sweetest man I've ever met."

"You ain't seen nothing, yet." I grinned, and my mind unfurled with the promise of many days, weeks and years of moments, gifts, experiences. Oh, how I'd spoil her. She'd never lack for attention, or for love.

"I baked you a cake." My brows shot up in question and she smiled. "Well, Muriel and I didn't bake it for you. We took it to the party, but I was bringing you some." She tilted her head to the side. "I lost it. On the island."

"Aah. Well. I'm sure the blue-footed boobies are enjoying the crumbs now. You can make me another sometime."

"I will. I promise. When you come to visit."

20

Three Months Later

ELLE

HE DREW MY EYE INSTANTLY, as he did every time. When Joe had asked me if he should cut his hair short, and shave off his beard, once he'd moved back to Seattle, I'd said, no. Keep them. So he had.

Of course he was much tidier now, and much to his chagrin and occasional discomfort, was required to wear shirts and shoes. At least when he was out and about. But he still cut an imposing figure, no matter that he wore a jacket, jeans and sneakers, drawing the admiring gaze of passing women like flies to honey, and not a few envious men.

He found me, and our eyes met, our wide smiles mirroring each other. I hurried along the arrivals corridor at Sea-Tac Airport, anxious to close the distance between us.

Unbelievably, both of our lives had been upturned in the past three months. Joe had pretty much packed up his home in Mexico, turning it into a vacation rental, and reintegrated back into his life in the States. It had been complicated. Mostly, he said, involving a lot of paperwork. And of course for him, the biggest difference was being able to work more closely with his company and all his employees, instead of at arms length. Luis's job description had changed the most.

Joe had leased a small, secluded waterfront house on Mercer Island, the quietest, most private setting he could find and still be close to his office and warehouse. And most days, he didn't leave it.

It was still hard for him, to be around a lot of people. He said his skin was thinner, and he'd lost the ability to deal with them easily. Very often he just tuned out, retreating into his own thoughts in silence.

Since my return home after the Christmas holiday, he'd flown, or driven, to see me in Vancouver a total of three times. And this was just my second trip down to see him in Seattle. That was quite a lot of togetherness for just three months. But somehow, whenever we parted, we both desperately needed to plan the next trip as soon as possible.

But despite the short time, and the newness of it all, the most important thing for both of us was being together again, for however short a time our busy lives permitted. For me, school set my schedule, so I was confined to weekends.

This time, I could stay a full week, since it was the school spring break, and we were both looking forward to the opportunity to relax into a string of days and nights in each other's company.

I passed the barrier and stepped up close to him, toe to toe, offering myself up for his touch.

"Hey, there, beautiful." He obliged by wrapping his arms around me, holding me snugly, and we breathed in the scent of the other. Relieved. He slipped my bag off my shoulder.

"Hi, you," I replied. He felt like home.

He kissed me briefly and turned, keeping his arm around me as we strode out together to his car.

"Have you cleared your schedule?" I asked.

"I absolutely have," he said, a smile in his voice. "I even stocked the kitchen. I don't plan to let you out of the house all week."

"So. You'll finally turn me into your captive sex slave," I teased, not at all worried about it. In fact, rather looking forward to it.

He looked both ways before leading me across the crosswalk to the parkade. "That's the plan; yes, ma'am."

I felt so safe tucked under his arm, I could have been floating a foot off the ground. I giggled, happiness filling me like a helium balloon, and he paused in the parkade to kiss me slowly. Once in his new Tesla, he laced our fingers together and didn't let go until we pulled into his driveway a half hour later.

We entered the foyer of his mid-century modern rancher and he unceremoniously dropped my bag, turned and pressed me against the side wall of the entry, kissing me sensually and thoroughly until my knees went weak with desire.

"So it begins," I murmured and wordlessly he picked me up and carried me down the hall to his bedroom, stripping me, tossing my clothes everywhere, intent and focussed.

"Elle. I missed you so much," he whispered, planting a trail of kisses from my lips to my shoulder, from my breasts to my belly and on.

"I can't believe how much I missed you," I replied, my hands dancing over his hard muscles, his broad contoured chest, his lean hard hip bones.

"I missed you more," he mumbled, his hungry mouth on my skin, his hands greedy.

Then we stopped speaking, so lost in touching each other, our gazes locked and adoring as we did what we did best. I knew it was early days for us yet. Our adoration for and obsession with each other could yet fade. But something about our connection felt fateful. So far, our love had only grown deeper. Being with him, I could easily imagine this being my forever, and Joe was forthright in his claims that it was just a matter of time. The logistics drove him crazy. He wanted it all now.

"I've wasted enough of my life," he said. "I don't want to be alone anymore."

Afterwards, he lay beside me, his one arm tucked under me, the other behind his head. "I'm so happy I get you all to myself for seven uninterrupted nights." I hummed contentedly, agreeing. "I don't think I'll even let you leave my bed."

"I might get hungry."

"I'll feed you," he said. "I'll cook for you."

"Do I get to shower?"

"No."

"No?" I lifted my head from the pillow to query him with my eyes.

He chuckled. "Well, yes, if you take me with you."

I kissed his beautiful, strong mouth and rested my head on his shoulder.

"I seriously miss you every moment I'm not with you. I think about you constantly. I'm even jealous of your students."

"I'll read you a story."

"Will you? Will it be a thriller?"

"I don't think so. You don't care for them, I hear."

"Something historical then?"

I shook my head. "No, contemporary."

"A romance?"

I nodded. "Mhm. I'll read you a love story. Something to warm your heart, and give you hope."

"My heart is quite warm already, actually, as well as other parts," He angled his body, casting a heavy leg over mine and rubbed his already reviving erection against me. "And I'm quite a hopeful guy, these days."

And we slipped wordlessly into lovemaking again, our eyes never leaving each other's, cresting softly when the intensity became too much. It was like breathing now, so natural being together. The safest, most comfortable place in the world.

He sighed and rolled off of me, and I hummed happily.

Lying together afterwards, staring at his ceiling, satisfied, spent, his arms behind his head, he began to hum a tune.

"Are you singing?"

He kept going, a little louder and then added the words. "Lavender's blue, dilly, dilly. Lavender's green. When I am king, dilly, dilly, you shall be queen."

I smiled and replied, softly, because I was shy about my singing voice, "Who told you so, dilly, dilly, who told you so?"

He turned his face toward me, whispering the next line in my ear. "'Twas my own heart, dilly, dilly, that told me so." He rolled back over me, framing me with his elbows, and my hands came up to caress his flexed biceps. He smiled.

"Hm, I love your muscles," I lifted my head to kiss his mouth, then kiss him on his shoulder, on the angry red scar of his last bullet wound that was slowly fading to pink.

He dropped his head to kiss my breast, my chin, the tip of my nose.

"I love all of you. Every bit."

"I love you too, darling, sweet, man."

He paused a moment, his adoring gaze sliding over my face as if he thought I were too good to be true. The feeling was mutual. "I think I'll keep you close forever."

Bonus Epilogue: Seven Months Later

ELLE

"HE'S HERE! There's the box truck," called Tannis from her position at the window.

My heart did a little double back flip, sending shivers and shimmers of excitement through my limbs and into my stomach like a fizz of champagne. No matter how many times I was reunited with Joe, I felt the thrill of it like the first time. Or maybe the second time, I amended, remembering how terrifying he was the *very* first time I saw him.

Laura set down her coffee cup and stood up from the sofa, stepping in front of me, taking my arms in her hands. "Are you excited?" Her grin was contagious, and I realized I'd lost my smile in the depth of my feelings.

I swallowed, struggling to speak through my thickened throat. "I'm...so..." My chin quivered, twisting my smile. Suddenly I was overcome. This was a reunion unlike any before, because this time, he'd be staying forever.

"You'd better pull yourself together or Joe will think you're sorry he's come."

I scoffed. "Shut up. You know I'm just so happy I can't contain my feelings."

She wrapped herself around me, squeezing and rocking me side to side. "I know, Ellie." Laughter huffed through her nose as Tannis joined us, encircling us both in her long, lean arms for a group hug, bouncing us up and down.

"I'm so stoked for you, Cuz."

"Thanks you two. I'm so grateful you're here to help. And that you'll both finally get a chance to know Joe better."

"Are you kidding me? Like we'd miss an opportunity to ogle your man," Tannis teased.

"That's not true." Laura jabbed Tannis in the arm. "But we are happy you two are finally moving in together."

Laura and Tannis had both met Joe on his previous visits north. But between my work and his, his stays were never long, and when he was here, we spent most of our time tangled up in each other, not socializing. In between, there'd been many life hurdles to overcome. Reintegrating Joe into his business life had been a long, slow process. His staff were all a bit dumbfounded that the mysterious, reclusive CEO of their company had suddenly reappeared. Many of the newer employees had never met him. They seemed to believe he actually existed.

And for him, the hands on, face-to-face reality of work had been both a thrill, and a challenge. His people skills were rusty. He tended to be silent and stoic, gruff and jumpy, or revert to speaking through Luis out of habit. Finally he became immersed in improvements and changes, stimulated by the dynamic exchange of input from his buyers and sellers, venturing into new marketplaces and shifting the focus of the products they imported.

At first, we were both busy with work. Then, during the summer months I got off from work, I'd spent longer stretches with him down in Seattle. Now as we eased into Fall, and another holiday season approached, we were in upheaval again. Through it all, though, he kept his sights on me. We spoke or texted continuously, and never went more than a week without a plan to see each other again. Somehow, we'd flowed effortlessly into this mutual absorption. This shared life. The suddenness of our meeting, parting and reunion seemed to have jogged something loose for both of us. We'd charged ahead into this relationship without reservations. It just felt right. And with each successive visit, our love and certainty had grown stronger. We wanted to be together. We were each other's family now. We had to find a way to make it work. And so that had become our mission.

The intercom buzzed, and all three of us jumped apart, laughing.

Laura hit the button and a few minutes later there was a light thump on the door.

Tannis swung it wide to reveal Joe, casual and handsome in a ball cap, a bright new white t-shirt stretching across his muscled chest, and soft grey sweat pants. He said he'd not quite got used to the confinement of jeans after years of having the air and sun on his skin. It was fine with me. He was gorgeous no matter what he wore. I was more excited by the prospect of waking up to his naked body in my bed every morning.

As if that's exactly what he were thinking, too, he swept me into his arms and kissed me ardently, and for a brief moment, we forgot we had an audience.

"Hi, there, Joe," Laura said as he finally let me slide down his hard, sexy body and released me onto wobbly legs.

I sighed and grinned at him in welcome. "Hello, handsome."

Joe smiled and greeted my besties, and we got to work unloading the van.

After countless trips up and down the elevator with a dolly stacked with boxes—Joe's rental place in Seattle had been furnished, so his belongings consisted of only personal items and keepsakes that had been in storage—we all sat down around the dining table with cold glasses of iced tea, catching our breath.

"When do you have to drop off the U-Haul?" I asked Joe.

"Before four-thirty." Joe dragged a hand over his damp brow, and raked it through his brown waves, drawing our collective gaze to his bulging bicep. I let my gaze linger a moment on his strong neck, and the droplet of preparation that trickled beneath the neckband of his shirt.

Then I smiled, kicking Tannis under the table to break the spell. "Down, girl. He's all mine."

Tannis burst into laughter. "I can look, can't I?"

I shot a glance to Laura, who had the grace to blush at her open admiration of Joe. "And you have a perfectly fine fiancé, Miss Laura."

She chuckled, her gaze cast down. "Of course I do. Sean's perfect. Just not..." She waved her hand vaguely in Joe's direction.

I no longer had cause to envy either my beautiful bestie Laura, nor my accomplished, ambitious cousin Tannis. Although I did sometimes wonder why Laura didn't sparkle with the same giddy bliss I felt, though she was planning her wedding with Sean next year. And Tannis, despite her considerable assets, never seemed to have time for men in her life. I had, amazingly, and perhaps against the odds, achieved my own happily ever after. I lifted my eyes to catch Joe's sparkling tropical blue gaze, and we locked together, the rest of the world fading away, as it always did, love flowing wordlessly between us. I felt my eyes tingle and swim with tears.

Joe winked, squeezed my hand in understanding, and said with a sigh, "I'd better shift these boxes around so we can move around up here. Then I'll take the truck back."

I glanced around our chaotic new condo with a sigh. Once we'd determined to live together, and Joe had come to the conclusion that running his company from Vancouver was just as simple as being in Seattle, and a far sight better than running it from Mexico, we'd started shopping for real estate. The two story penthouse on the Cole Harbour waterfront suited us perfectly. Joe liked to be able to walk out the door, shop at the market or go to a show without having to deal with driving. He really hated driving in the city, and though I was fine with it, my drive to work took less than a half hour. The water and mountain views were spectacular, and our large rooftop deck, made it feel like we were able to live outdoors as much as in. My plan was to make the apartment and deck feel as jungle-like as possible, though so far I had only acquired one large potted palm, and a lemon tree, along with a new sofa. A far cry from Yelapa.

From here Joe could walk to the harbour air terminal and fly directly to Seattle harbour in less than an hour. In an emergency, Luis could come and pick him up in the helicopter. It took longer than that to commute from the Valley.

"Shall I order Szechuan for dinner while you're out?"

"Sure." Joe leaned in to kiss me. "Anything but tacos, Angel."

I laughed. He'd actually really been enjoying the novelty of varied cuisines since coming back. And between Seattle and Vancouver, we had the best of the world at our fingertips.

"Yum. Sounds good to me." Tannis jumped up. "Tell me where you want stuff and I'll help." She was a wonder of strength, agility and energy, with her long lean limbs, whereas I was ready to flop on the sofa with a glass of wine. But, there was still work to be done.

Another hour and a half later, and Joe's stuff had been sorted and stacked in the spare room, the home office, or our bedroom, and he left to return the rental truck. The unpacking and organizing would wait for another day. While Joe was away, we three women sat side by side on the new long grey sectional sofa that had been delivered last week, drinking that wine I'd been craving.

"To your new life together." Laura raised her glass, and Tannis and I brought ours in to toast. "I hope you and Joe will be very happy together, and that wedding invitations will be forthcoming." She smirked.

I smiled to myself. Joe and I had talked about marriage, before deciding to make the move and live together. We'd agreed, it'd be nice, someday, to formally tie the knot. Maybe more for me, who'd never been married. But at our age, it was something we'd rather do quietly, without fanfare, maybe even on the beach in Mexico, if I could persuade my parents to fly down.

A much higher priority, after moving, was to focus on getting pregnant. Our last tryst on the beach in Yelapa had not resulted in a pregnancy. And strangely, we'd both confessed to being a teensy bit disappointed. So now that we were settling down, trying for a family together was our top to-do, even if we needed a bit of help. And toward that end, the stress and expense of a wedding was off the table. But all of that was a secret for now.

"I'll drink to cohabiting. No need for that other stuff," Tannis declared, slurping a big sip of red wine, then gesturing at Laura. "And you know they'll be happy. That man can't keep his eyes, or his hands, off of her."

We sat back, and I sighed happily. "Thanks, guys. I can only wish this much happiness for each of you. I love you both."

"And we love you right back," Tannis sang.

The buzzer announced the arrival of our food, and we'd barely begun laying out the *Mapo Doufu* and *Gongbao Jiding* on the table, and setting out bowls and chopsticks before Joe had returned.

With a quick kiss he said, "Get started. I'll just have a quick shower and be right out."

"Need any help with that?" I murmured, for his ears only.

He smirked. "Maybe we can christen the new shower together later tonight." And he kissed me again, deeply, and with intention, and a shiver of anticipation ran over me like a river of silk.

A few minutes later, he joined us at the table, and we all dug into the delicious food with gusto.

"So, you guys," I said, after slaking my hunger, sitting back and glancing around the table. "Any plans for the holidays? Joe and I are thinking of heading down to Mexico for a month or so of sun and surf. It's our first year."

"Oh, that'll be lovely, Elle," Laura said between mouthfuls. "Nice for you two to return and just enjoy yourselves without, you know, death threats."

"How about you and Sean join us? And you Tannis? Wouldn't it be fun?"

Tannis groaned. "Oh, wow. That would be nice. Sadly I'm stuck going on a family vacation to Costa Rica this year. We're flying down before American Thanksgiving to meet up with Dad's Florida cousins, and staying together in this jungle resort Dad booked. I'm afraid there's no getting out of it for me."

"I don't know why Costa Rica makes you sad, Tan." I said. "That sounds like a fantastic escape."

She made a sad face and hummed. "Oh, family stuff. I wish I could get away from them sometimes. Dad's hot to see monkeys and coatimundis and tropical birds and stuff. All I can think of are the spiders and shit." She shuddered. "Anyway, I'll have heaps of studying and papers to write even though we're away."

I mirrored her pout. "Maybe next time, then. Joe and I really want to show you his place."

"You're welcome anytime," Joe added. "Even if we're not there."

"And I can't wait to see it. Sounds amaze-balls. How about you Lo? Mexico this year?"

"I'm sorry, too. But Sean's family has been planning a cruise.

Same as you, Tannis. A big family thing, kind of an engagement party combined with his Dad's sixtieth-fifth birthday and, I don't know, I think they're celebrating the merger, too. It's kind of a big deal."

"Sounds fancy. Where are you cruising?" I asked.

"The Mediterranean, apparently. I don't know the details yet. But same, no escape for me." She shook her head, while I thought a Mediterranean cruise sounded just fine, too. But only if Joe came with me.

"Well, maybe if we plan ahead, we can all fly down to Yelapa for a little beach wedding the following Christmas," Joe dead-panned, and I closed my eyes, smiling and shaking my head. Okay, not a secret.

Eventually, after Joe had been teased and admired for his romantic inclinations, Laura and Tannis said their good-byes, and it was just Joe and me, in our new home alone at last.

"Do you even know where your toothbrush is?" I asked from my cozy place tucked under his arm on the sofa. "I'm worn out from moving boxes around. I'm getting sleepy."

He chuckled. "I do actually. I made sure to pack a little bag of essentials in case everything got scrambled." Which, glancing around our cluttered place, it had.

"Wise man," I hummed, letting my heavy eyelids drop.

After looking at me for a long minute in silence, he lifted his arm from around my shoulders and gently pushed me back to lie on the sofa, then angled over me, kissing my lips gently, then nuzzling my neck with his beard, kissing my ear and cheek, sliding down my collarbone to plant a kiss between my breasts while sliding my shirt up over them and tossing it to the floor. His own shirt soon followed.

"What about our shower?" I smiled and looked down at his disheveled waves.

Pausing near my belly button, his fingers hooked into the waistband of my soft yoga pants, he looked up, meeting my gaze, and I marvelled at his beautiful blue eyes, sparkling with mischief and invitation like the tropical sea, his handsome face, his broad shoulders flanking my body, and sighed happily. He murmured against my skin, "It'll be there tomorrow. Just close your eyes, love, and I'll kiss you good-night right here."

Then he continued his slow descent to my hips, pulling my pants with him as he went. Then, as they were exposed to the air, and his hot touch, my trembling inner thighs, planting kisses on the tender inside of my knees as he spread my legs and sank back to my centre.

"Home, at last," he whispered against my tender flesh.

"Oh!" I had to agree.

***

THE END

DID you enjoy Elle and Joe's Christmas adventure? Be sure to watch for cousin Tannis' Christmas story next!

HERE'S another fun read by USA Today Best-selling author MaryAnn Clarke. Start reading Book 1 in the new Most UNLIKELY To series: The Reporter's UNLIKELY Reunion and meet these friends from Port Camosun at their ten year reunion. Get it here: https://www.amazon.com/MaryAnn-Clarke/e/B01KPSGXNO

Sample Chapter of The Reporter's UNLIKELY Reunion

Julian

Ten years ago, my life plan had been simple. I knew exactly who I was, where I was going, and what I wanted.

I was Julian Michaels, an easy-going, third-generation chicken farmer, and I'd be married to my high school sweetheart with two, maybe three kids, I figured. A dog, of course. A simple, pleasant life stretching as far into the future as I could see.

Then everything came crashing down. My life, my future, my dreams, my faith in humanity, and my self belief.

I learned that nothing is simple; you can't ever really know or trust anyone—including yourself—and life was random. It was best to take things one day at a time. Be adaptable. Take pleasure in simple things.

Even so, I wasn't prepared.

"Julian! Julian!" A chorus of female voices rose to greet me the moment I walked through Millhouse Coffee. Collectively, the voices belonged to two of my oldest and dearest friends: Quinn, the proprietor of the café, and Deanna, my social media mentor.

I'd known them since middle school. They were two-fifths of a dynamic group of clever, popular, can-do girlfriends ironically known as the Kickass Chicks. Quinn, Deanna, and Rainy—who was at work—were the only three that stayed in our hometown, and at the moment were the core organizing committee of our tenth high school reunion. I was a mere hanger-on, their mascot if you will. Also, their caterer.

They leapt from their chairs, swarming me as I strode toward the table where their lists and spreadsheets, seating arrangements and menus were spread. I felt my neck and face heat with embarrassment as they batted their eyelashes in slow-mo, made smooching faces, and fake swooned all over me.

"I love you, Julian!"

"You're so sexy, Julian!"

"Julian, will you marry me?"

"Geroff!" I chuckled good-naturedly, peeling their arms from my neck and pushing them away as they giggled. I was a lucky man to have so many warm and true friends, and beautiful women to boot—inside and out.

I could hardly blame them for the teasing. My newest Instagram Live had gone viral, and my following had grown by ten thousand over the week, thanks to the coaching and technical support of Deanna the social media queen. Or influencer, as she was known, with the 748,000 followers of her Dee+Dun Beauty and Wellness profile. I wondered if the explosion of follows for my farm and food page and gaga girl fans qualified me as an influencer now too. All for tromping around my farm with my dog Finnigan and my goats and chickens like the hick that I was. What a weird world we live in.

"Your following, dude!" said Deanna, giving me a side hug.

"Thanks to you. You really are brilliant, Dee. I'm over the moon."

Swooning girl fans who thought I was some kind of rustic

sex symbol was not what I'd expected from the new cooking and sustainable food campaign, nor what I signed up for. I felt awkward AF, but if the attention got me the audience I sought for my brand, and the sponsorships and partnerships I needed to advance my cause—and pay for my animals' feed—I could hardly complain. My actual cost of living was very low, since I essentially lived off my land as much as possible.

They sat down and I joined them, sweeping their papers aside and setting down my cloth-covered tin tray in the centre of the table.

"Ooh! What's this?" asked Deanna, pinching the edge of the cloth to peek underneath. Deanna's diet was too health conscious and frou-frou to allow her to enjoy my cooking fully, and Quinn had rather conservative tastes, though she wholeheartedly supported my sustainable, local approach. But I made sure to include all their needs and preferences when planning the menu, as they were a rather spot-on avatar for my target audience. And I aimed to please.

I swatted her hand away. "Hold on a sec. Where's Rainy?"

"Running late."

She was the most adventurous foodie of the group and loved to sample every new thing I came up with. The highly anticipated event was tomorrow night, and it was my food that would grace the buffet and circulate among the crowd. The food had to be superb, brilliant, and eye-catching, as well as on message. I might be attending the reunion mainly to spend time with my closest friends and reconnect with a few old ones, but I had an ulterior motive.

"Have you got the final numbers for us?"

Deanna pulled her hand back, dragged her laptop closer and clicked. "Yes. There were a few last-minute responses." She scanned her screen. "We heard from Alex whatsit. He is coming after all and he's bringing his husband."

"Any more?"

"Mhm. The four from Boston confirmed. Elsa from Montreal is coming. Dean and his wife from up in Prince George are coming down. Oh! I got a call from James Reynold's mom. He died! She just heard about the reunion and finally got back to me."

"Another one to add to the deceased poster," murmured Quinn, rummaging under the stacks of papers and jotting his name on a list.

I vaguely recalled James. "The theatre guy? With the curly hair?"

Quinn added, "Voted Most Likely To End Up on a Soap Opera." She frowned down at her list, scratching her pen through a line.

"Wasn't he friends with Tate?"

"Yeah, that's what I remember, too," Quinn said, her bright features falling. "They were in the theatre club together. I wonder if Tate knows."

Deanna chewed her lip. "She said it was cancer. Throat cancer. How cruel is that?"

"Fuck cancer," grumbled Quinn. "Want a coffee, Julian?"

"Nah, thanks. I've gotta run. My buddy Arnie is delivering an alpaca this afternoon. I have to get back to the farm."

"A what? Alpaca? Is that like a... like a llama?"

I laughed. "Yeah. Sorta."

"Why on earth would you—?"

I brushed her question aside with a shake of my head. I didn't want the hassle of learning about a new species, but Arnie was adamant.

"And Jeannie? She still coming?" I turned to Quinn, raising my brows in question. Quinn was the only one who Jeannie had stayed in touch with since grad.

Deanna's face lit up. "I am so excited to see her. I can't believe she's not been back once in ten years."

Quinn gave me her sedate trademark smile, and I caught the undertone of sympathy beneath. She knew I'd never ask directly about Ruby, and that Jeannie was a kind of stand-in for my perverse self-indulgent curiousity about the missing fifth member of the clique. "Jeannie was due to arrive from Toronto tonight. But there was some work thing, and she had to reschedule her flight for tomorrow. It's up in the air but she's still hoping to make it in time."

"She'd better goddamwell make it," Deanna grumbled, making a pouty face. "It won't be a reunion at all without her. I'm still mad at her for cutting us all off."

"Not all of us," I said, elbowing Quinn, who shrugged, pulling a face. Being in Jeannie's confidence, she knew things that she hinted at but never shared. Quinn was like a vault.

We fell silent, as though we all were thinking the same thought at the same moment. Which, undoubtedly, we were. It wouldn't be the same without Ruby either, but nobody expected Ruby to come. And they didn't talk about her in front of me, anyway.

Deanna cleared her throat to break the awkward silence. "So. The final numbers are here. A hundred and twenty-six, give or take. Is that close enough for you?"

"Sure. Anyway, I had some ingredient substitutions and re-jigged a few of the appetizers, so I brought some samples for your approval."

"Ooh. Taste test." Quinn rubbed her hands together, licking her lips.

I swept away the covering cloth with a flourish to reveal my latest creations. I pointed to one. "Harissa grilled baby lamb on sumac flatbreads. You should get a little kick and a gorgeous depth of flavour from the roasted spices, but nothing to knock your socks off."

Tentatively, Quinn plucked one stack off of the tray and

popped it whole into her mouth. She closed her eyes and savoured it, humming. "Nice."

"Caramelized shallots on slices of gluten-free Hasselback Jerusalem artichokes for you Deanna."

Deanna picked a sample and peered at it for a moment before touching it with the tip of her tongue. She liked the colour and shape of things as much as their taste and so I'd decorated the tops with a dollop of Creme Fraiche and a pretty sprig of chervil. I thought she'd like that, and as she smiled at it and took a dainty bite, I knew she did. She chewed thoughtfully, and I watched her eyes register the lovely silky texture combined with the chewiness of the artichokes. Another winner.

"Next," Quinn said, waiting for the introduction that always preceded my food.

I picked up one of the dessert items. "How about something sweet, Quinny? This one's maple sugar rhubarb mousse in a cardamom crisp, with wild strawberries and a caramel halo." Quinn's eyes lit up and she enthusiastically gave that a go. I sat back, watching them crunch and chew, listening to their moans of delight, knowing I'd knocked it out of the park.

Without warning, Deanna lurched forward with a guttural noise, her big, dark eyes bulging at something over my shoulder.

Deanna clutched at my sleeve as Quinn followed her gaze. As I went to turn around, Quinn grabbed a paper napkin and spit the contents of her mouth into her hand.

What the hell?

"What's wrong? Does it taste bad? What is it?" Had I mixed up sugar and salt? Accidentally dropped chili pepper into the mousse? I didn't do stuff like that. I was exacting and careful; some might say, too precise.

She frowned and hissed, "Don't turn around. Don't turn around."

Deanna let out a long plaintive cry like someone had stepped on a cat. Of course I turned, because whatever had caused this uproar in my girls had to be faced.

Of all the things or people I expected to see entering the café when I turned, it was not Ruby.

My head roared with a whooshing, tidal wave of blood; burning, anguished tears shot from my tear ducts as my throat seized up.

"Did she contact you? Did you know?"

"No. No, I never got a reply to the invitation."

"I thought she was in Afghanistan."

"No, it was Azerbaijan."

I heard the halting exchange between the girls through the thunder in my ears.

I squeezed my eyes closed, opened them wide, shut them again. Surely my mind was playing tricks on me. I'd imagined I'd seen my Ruby a million times over the years. Here on the streets downtown, and even in London, Paris, Rome, and New York; there were times when I was convinced that the person I saw in a crowded restaurant on the sidewalk up ahead was Ruby. But it never was. This, my pounding heart jammed into my throat told me, was undoubtedly Ruby.

Suddenly, we were all on our feet. I don't remember rising. Everything happened at once, in a staccato rhythm.

Deanna rushed forward calling her name, then stopped and glanced back at me, uncertain. Quinn stayed by my side, her fingers digging into my bicep, as though she thought I might topple over without her support. And I might have. I still might.

"Ruby? Is that really you?" Deanna stepped forward.

Ruby, for it truly was her, stood blinking at the bunch of us, disoriented too. Did she come in here by accident? Her lips opened to speak, but she stalled. She reached a hand out, and Deanna clasped then released it.

"Hey… wow… guys. I…" Her gaze skipped across each of us, but kept bouncing back to me, locking on me. As our gazes met, her pupils huge and black, I felt as though I'd fallen into deep space; she seemed as disoriented as I felt.

Deanna stepped back while Quinn released my arm at last, shoving me forward. I stumbled. I didn't know what she wanted me to do. What was I supposed to do?

"Jules?" Ruby's voice reached me, scratchy and faint, like a bad recording. "I didn't expect to see you here. Mom told me about Quinn's new place and I…"

No words came when I tried to find them. Something cottony closed my throat. My eyes burned and my skin was hot and tingling. Confused, I turned to look at Quinn and Deanna. They'd retreated, huddled together like nervous puppies.

"Jules?" Ruby stepped closer and closer. Ten inches away, then eight. I could smell her. Feel her breath on my face. She lifted a hand as if to touch me, but stopped mid air and let it drop. She knew better than to try, this woman who destroyed me. She was part stranger, part lover, part ruination, and it was hella confusing; a storm of emotions swirled inside me.

But then she did touch me. First her palms landed featherlight on my chest, as if gauging my temperature, like a hot stove. Then her arms slid up and around my neck, grabbing fistfuls of my shirt and pulling me closer, tipping her face to the crook of my neck, grazing it with a feather touch. The familiar scent of her, dark chocolate and the cinnamon spice of carnations that I'd loved so much, swamped my senses.

In a flash, my body remembered what I'd fought ten years to forget. The silky feel of her thick hair and smooth skin against mine. My fingers tingled, and my arms ached to grab her and pull her into me, hold her tight. I feathered my fingertips on her back, and felt her ribs and vertebrae jutting, strange in their gaunt hardness. But I could go no further, enveloped by her trembling breath and crushed by the sound of my own heartbeat in my ears.

Suddenly we were at the centre of a frenzied group hug, the other girls rushing us and twining their arms around both of us. Pressed closer to Ruby, our chests, bellies, hips, and thighs connected, a fever of familiar desire washed over me; my body temperature shot up as my skin screamed and nerve endings lit up. Blood surged to my groin in a tidal wave of sexual reverberations. I tried to pull back but was locked into the embrace, painfully conscious of my swelling groin.

They must have all realized they were crowding us at the same moment, because the group broke apart and everyone teetered back a step. My head was on fire.

I drew a breath. Some shards of sense cut through the fog. Finally, I found my voice, a choked, stiff, drowning voice. "Are you here for the reunion?"

She winced and swayed on her feet. Her head tilted to the left. "No. No, I didn't know. My mom and dad just told me about it." Her shoulder hitched up. "That's why I came looking for Quinn."

I said nothing. Did I honestly expect she'd look me up first? Or at all?

She looked great. Fantastic. Strong, lean, and tanned, her brown hair streaked with gold. Of course, I'd seen her on TV. We all had. So it's not like the changes wrought by ten years in her field should shock me. But they did all the same. In the flesh she looked tired, weathered. Not the incandescent, nubile Ruby of our youth. Tiny lines flared out from the corners of her hazel eyes, and cut into the sides of her full mouth. It was a hard life she'd chosen. I knew that. Still, she was as beautiful to me as ever.

I reached up to rub the back of my head, staring down at my rubber work boots, now painfully aware that I'd come in directly from the farm. I was in my rattiest t-shirt and scarf, my baggiest work pants. I never fussed about clothes anymore, but my skin crawled now with self-consciousness. A deep, crippling sense of my inadequacy swamped me.

"Are all of you going to the reunion?" Ruby finally asked, scanning the group.

"Of course we are. We organized it. And now so are you!" squeaked Deanna, leaping closer. I just kept staring at her, as blood roared in my ears to the sound of her name. Ruby, Ruby, Ruby.

"You're going?" Ruby's big green-bronze eyes circled my features, as if she too were taking the measure of time since we'd last been together.

"Ah… nooo, actually. Nope." Tugging on my scarf, I shoved my hands in my pockets and stepped back to give myself a bit of space. I registered the sharp intake of breath behind me. "Have an alpaca to unpack. Got to get it… settled." This couldn't be happening. I took a step to the side, clenching my hands into fists, and angled my shoulder towards her—like a bull intent on plowing through a fence. Anything to stop me from wrapping her in a crushing embrace, burying my face in her hair, drawing the scent of her skin into my lungs like a life-giving elixir.

"You are too going, Julian." Quinn's quiet voice came right behind me. "You have to go. Everyone expects you."

I twisted to glare at her. "No. Can't make it. Sorry." I turned back to Ruby. "You should though. Since you're back. Everyone will be so excited to see you." My God, I have to get out of here. I stepped around her, forcing myself to put one foot in front of the other until I found myself on the sidewalk out in front of the café. The warm summer air washed over me like a silken veil, waking me up from a dream. A volcano of emotion erupted from somewhere deep inside me; I felt like I was on fire. I had to get away, and fast.

Though anguish and horrible humiliation, and latent rage

swirled together in my gut, all my nerve endings stubbornly insisted on standing up together and singing a high clear note like a choir.

Ruby was back.

***

End of sample

Keep reading The Reporter's UNLIKELY Reunion.

Get it here: https://www.amazon.com/MaryAnn-Clarke/e/B01KPSGXNO

About the Author

MaryAnn Clarke ~ USA Today Bestselling author MaryAnn Clarke is a Chatelaine Grand Prize winner and Next Generation Indie Book Award finalist for The Art of Enchantment, first in the Life is a Journey series about young women on journeys abroad who discover themselves and fall in love while getting embroiled in someone else's problems. Her Having it All series is about professional women struggling to balance the challenge and fulfillment of their careers with their search for identity, love, family and home.

Always eager to fill blank pages and empty canvases with ideas swirling in her head, MaryAnn set out to write emotionally engaging stories that walk a tightrope between intelligent Women's Fiction and heart-warming Romance.

A socially awkward polymath with ASD who studied Fine Arts, Urbanism, Architecture and Gerontology at university on both coasts of Canada, she turned to her first love, writing stories, when she realized she could have more fun with fewer rules to follow. When not writing, she meditates while hiking wooded mountain trails, does yoga and Pilates to fend off decrepitude, reads eclectically, contemplates wormholes, experiments with painting abstract expressionism, kills plants and tries not to burn dinner while solving her next plot problem. Now that her chick has flown the coop, Clarke lives on beautiful Vancouver Island, Canada with her husband and cats. Although she knows she lives in Paradise, she still loves travelling the world in search of romance, art, good food and new story ideas.

Get MaryAnn's newsletter and never miss a new release!

Want to receive a FREE book? Join MaryAnn's mailing list to get all new and exclusive Single Dad in Studio 7D. Stay in touch to hear book news, special deals and updates about her new series release schedule.

You can read more about MaryAnn, her books and ideas that strike her fancy at www.maryannclarkescott.com.

FIND ALL OF HER BOOKS ON AMAZON AT
https://www.amazon.com/MaryAnn-Clarke/e/B01KPSGXNO

WANT TO CONNECT WITH ME?
www.maryannclarkescott.com
maryann@maryannclarkescott.com

Subscribe & Follow MACS!
www.maryannclarkescott.com
Question? Fan mail? Sure, you can reach me here.

Also by MaryAnn Clarke

The Reporter's UNLIKELY Reunion

The Phoenix's UNLIKELY Prodigy

Be Mine This Time

Making Room For You

Before You Knew Me

The Art of Enchantment

A Forged Affair

Single Dad in Studio 7D

Coming Soon

The Feminist's UNLIKELY Fiancé

Book, Line & Tinker

Running From Christmas: Book 2 of Off The Grid Christmas